WRITERS REPUBLIC

WRITERS REPUBLIC L.L.C.
515 Summit Ave. Unit R1
Union City, NJ 07087, USA

Website: *www.writersrepublic.com*
Hotline: *1-877-656-6838*
Email: *info@writersrepublic.com*

Ordering Information:
Quantity sales. Special discounts are available on quantity purchases by corporations, associations, and others. For details, contact the publisher at the address above.

Library of Congress Control Number: 2023930254
ISBN-13:   979-8-88810-018-9   [Paperback Edition]
                  979-8-88810-019-6   [Digital Edition]

Rev. date: 12/21/2022

The Wedding This Summer

HARRIETTE PATRICK BARRON

This novel is dedicated to everyone who have experienced joy and sadness in their life. I also want people over sixty-five to know that your family, your church, and your community need your strength and wisdom more now than ever. I hope that you will find new vitality by reading this novel. I hope that every person, their parents, and their grandparents will read this book. Let's appreciate our loved ones while they are still here. I also want to dedicate this novel to Mrs. Toneal M. Jackson and Ms. Amanda Alexander. Both of you were my inspiration to write this novel. Amanda inspired one of the most powerful characters in this novel. I am proud of the woman that you have become. Mrs. Toneal M. Jackson told me that I had more in me after I thought I had nothing left to say. Hygeia Bell Davis Patrick is my mother. She inspired my main character along with my four aunts. As life would have it, my husband and I, became his grandmother's caretaker after I nearly completed this novel. She was later placed on hospice in our small home. This novel came alive and I walked through what I had already written. Thanks to Erma Delores Dickey (Grand, Grand) for giving me the honor of caring for you during your final days on this earth.

Contents

Chapter 1

Days of Thunder

First Sergeant James Cook had just lain down after a long day of training his new crew of wide-eyed marines. He looked up at the ceiling and smiled thinking of his beautiful wife and two young sons.

"So sorry to bother you, Sergeant, but you have a phone call," said a corporal knocking on his door.

"Who could be calling me this late?"

"Sergeant Cook, my name is Dr. Guys. It's been a few years since we spoke. Do you remember me?"

"Of course, I do, How are you doing, Doctor?" James couldn't forget Dr. Guys because he had been such a huge part of his family's lives.

"Your wife is very ill and . . ." The doctor explained that he was placing his wife on hospice. "There is nothing else we can do for her."

"Wait, what? Back up, Doctor, what are you talking about? Carolyn has been in remission for three years. What happened?" James was blindsided by the call.

"Carolyn came to see me a few months back because she wasn't feeling well. During her examination, we discovered that the cancer had come back with a vengeance."

"Oh no." The latest round of chemotherapy was unsuccessful, and her time was quickly running out.

"We have tried all types of experimental treatment, but nothing has worked for your wife. I am so sorry. I thought she would have told you, but I don't think she has dealt with it herself. How soon can you come?" asked Dr. Guys.

Although he had been away a few times during their marriage, James couldn't even think of a future without his wife. James told them that he had to put in the proper paperwork with the Marines, but he would be there as soon as possible.

As a marine, he had long been trained on how to handle life-threatening situations. However, breast cancer was the most horrible enemy he had ever encountered. It had no remorse, no concern, and no discrimination for anyone.

Carolyn and First Sergeant James Cook sat enjoying their picnic on a warm August day. He had been on tour in South Korea for an entire year. Now he was home, and the love between them was stronger than ever. Both of them smiled watching their two sons pour warm sand over each other's head. "Those two are going straight to the tub when we get home," said James. The tired mother leaned her head back and listened to the crunchy leaves race across the grass.

"Carolyn, I still think it's too warm for you to be out here."

She gave a faint grin at her husband and clutched his hand. "I know, but I want to watch my boys play for a few more minutes, okay?" She talked him into taking her and the boys on a picnic.

"Okay, babe, whatever you want." James could see that her bony arms were getting weak from fanning herself with her sun hat. "Babe, you are really sweating. Let me do that for you," said James, taking the makeshift fan. Most of the South was hot in the summertime; but the scorching heat in Jefferson, Texas, was downright brutal.

Life had taken a toll on her body, and she was diagnosed a few years after they got married. It had been three years since she got to ring the bell at her oncologist's office. Although she had two breasts removed in her first bout with the disease, she still managed to give birth to twins a year later.

It was a breezy warm day for the children to come out and play. Carolyn jiggled her glass full of clanging ice cubes.

"I guess that's my sign to pour you a cold glass of sweet tea." Her husband noticed how his wife kept rubbing her bald head. "Why do you keep rubbing your head? Your hair is gone, but you are still the same person. I keep telling you that."

"I know, but I don't feel the same." Over the past few months, her long thick waist-length black hair had fallen out due to her most recent treatments. "My hair and eyebrows are both gone too," she said while rubbing her bald head. Carolyn had been so stunning that she had been offered a modeling contract after high school. She had even won the Miss Jefferson Beauty Pageant during her senior year.

"Darling, you are as beautiful today as you were at the wedding eight years ago. You remember that long tight white dress you had on. Girl, I almost died right there in the church," he said.

James was incredibly nervous about his sweating wife sitting in the sun for so long, but he loved to see her so happy. They had been at the park for about two hours when James looked over at his wife and noticed that she battled to breathe. "We need to leave. Come on, boys, let's go."

Later that evening, James spotted Carolyn grabbing the place where her breasts had once been. "I'm putting the boys to bed, then I'm coming back to help you get comfortable."

Carolyn frowned at James. "No, let me put them to bed. I will manage." She tried to bathe them, but she stumbled and nearly passed out trying to bend down beside the bathtub.

"Babe, you go rest, I got this," said James, putting bubbles in the bathwater.

Royce and William ran down the hallway naked after James gave them their bath. In the past, their mother would laugh and chase them down the hallway; but this time, she could not. Royce's father sat him on his mother's bony lap. Carolyn smiled as she slowly put on his Batman pajamas. James fought to put on William's Superman pajamas, but he finally got them on.

"We finally got those two little stinkers to bed," said the exhausted father, quietly closing their room door.

Around midnight, James sat up and looked around the room due to being startled by what sounded like pebbles hitting his window. It was hailing with a vengeance. "Babe, I can't breathe! I can't breathe." Not only was she grabbing her chest, but James could see that she was turning pale.

"I'm calling 911!"

"No, my way, James. I want to go on my own terms. You promised. Let's take one last ride. Please," she cried, barely breathing. He hesitated due to the hailing and thunder outside.

"Carolyn, it's time to go."

"Honey, let me talk to the boys one last time."

Wiping his mother's tears, Royce said, "Mommy cry. Why Mommy cry?"

William didn't say anything. Instead, he just laid his head on his mother's lap and hugged her knees.

"Boys, Mommy is going to the doctor, and I may not be back. I love you so much that it pains my heart that I will not see you become the men that I know you are going to be. I want you to know that your mommy fought to stay here with you!" Carolyn screamed into her napkin as her nose began to bleed. "I fought so hard to stay alive for both of you."

James made arrangements for Reverend Leroy Storm, Carolyn's pastor, and his wife, Mary, to come over and stay with the boys for a while.

"Pastor Storm and his wife are going to take care of you until your daddy gets back. Please remember that I will always be with you." James picked up William and asked, "Do you remember Regina?"

The toddler whispered, "No."

"William, she is coming to take you to her house in the morning." None of the adults liked the plan to separate the boys, but James didn't want the Storms to be overwhelmed with two toddlers. Carolyn had another stack of letters and pictures for James's cousin Regina Cook. The worried mother painfully coughed into her napkin until her shaking voice would no longer allow her to speak. Tears welled up in her eyes, and her frail five-foot-nine, one-hundred-twenty-pound frame shook. She tried to take in more air, but she could not. Whispering in First Lady Storm's ear, Carolyn handed her a stack of letters. Even James did not see what his wife passed to Mary.

"Give this to Royce and William when they are ready, okay?" she whispered.

"Okay, Carolyn, you know I will," cried Mary.

Pastor Storm carefully took Royce from his mother's frail lap. He reached for his mother, and he began to cry as she did not reach for him.

"Come on, babe, let's go." Although James was a strong military man, he could not even look at the agony in his son's eyes.

Carolyn had been the strongest soldier that he had ever seen.

"I wanted to fight harder, but I didn't have anything left."

"Baby, you fought harder than any soldier that I've ever seen."

"Babe, we almost beat it, didn't we?"

"Yes, you almost did," cried James, wiping his silent tears away. There were no more words to be said. James patted Carolyn's hand as she tearfully looked outside the car window.

"I still think we should have called the ambulance to get you." He didn't hear any response from his wife.

"Carolyn! Stay with me, babe."

Her thin frame kept leaning over, and her bones would no longer support her. She was going on her own terms.

She fought a good fight. The soldier known as Carolyn Cook lost the battle to the enemy called cancer just five minutes before they made it to the hospice center.

James felt as if his life had suddenly come crashing down. Grief was attempting to take a hold of him, but it had to wait. Now there was the business of funeral planning and childcare. Like a robot, he calmly signed all the papers that allowed the funeral home to take Carolyn's body. It was a struggle, and he struggled to admit that he thought about buying a bus ticket and leaving town. Not only did he want to go AWOL from the military, he wanted to go AWOL from his two young children. Everything in him wanted to run for cover from the war raging in his mind. He had phone calls to make, but how could he? He couldn't even speak due to his heart being so heavy.

Come on, man, you are a soldier. Get it together. Although it was difficult, James picked up the phone and made the first phone call. "Pastor, I just called to tell you that Carolyn passed away."

"James, I'm so sorry. Do you want us to keep Royce for a few days? I know you have a lot of preparations to do. I'll tell my wife."

James agreed that he had a lot of work to do and had to find a nice funeral home for his wife. James was silent on the phone.

"Son, are you there?" asked Reverend Storm.

"Oh yes, I'm sorry. Just a little overwhelmed. Will you call Cousin Regina to see if she will keep William for a few days?"

Pastor Storm agreed to pass the news on to Regina.

I promised Carolyn that I would take care of them. I can't let her down . . . I can't let them down. Grief began eating away at his heart, and all his emotions came rushing out. Sliding down the hospital wall, James wailed and sobbed as if he had been defeated by a vicious enemy.

"Sir, are you okay?" asked the hospice chaplain. James was so overwhelmed that he couldn't even lift his head to see who was talking to him. Since he could not pull James up, the chaplain slid down right beside him. "Son, can I pray for you?" he asked.

"Man, you can do whatever you want. I could use some help right now. Everything in me wants to run, but I can't," wailed James. Although he was a strong soldier, he fell into the arms of a man that he didn't know. Finally, looking up through his tears, James looked into the eyes of an elderly chaplain. "Please don't tell anyone that I fell into the arms of an old man." He snickered while blowing his nose.

"Son, you have no idea how many men I have held and hugged. I'm a chaplain, and my job is to comfort and pray for those in need. I have a son about your age, and he still gets plenty of hugs from me."

James was slightly embarrassed, but he accepted the comfort and the Christ that the chaplain offered.

He also received the strength he needed to complete the funeral arrangements for Carolyn and make arrangements for the care of his sons. He was able to make a family plan with the Marines and looked forward to returning home in six months. Due to Cousin Regina being his only relative, he left the boys in her custody while he finished his six-month tour.

First Sergeant Cook crossed off each date on his calendar. Each red mark indicated that he was one day closer to being discharged back to the family that he loved. Training bright-eyed marines helped him feel that he was leaving the armed forces in good hands. His group of guys was special to him, and oddly enough they prayed together each day. They conducted all types of military exercises and war preparedness.

James read his letters and showed his pictures to the guys that had no family. His faith in God had also strengthened during his tour, and he loved praying with the chaplain each day. It was obvious that he struggled after the death of his wife, but he still had some hope for his children. "Now, I know that I can do all things with God's help," wrote James in a letter to Pastor Storm. James called Regina to check on the boys. "I can't wait to see how big my boys have gotten. I'm going to be right in time for their third birthday. I got them two huge toy helicopters with pilots inside. They are going to flip when they see it." He couldn't wait to see four small hazel eyes that were the only thing left from his beautiful bride.

James felt so glad knowing that he would soon be reunited with his sons. Love welled up inside of him as he dropped their birthday gifts in the mail. He imagined him and his boys running through the field playing with their gifts. James was going to yell, "Okay, guys, prepare for liftoff!" Royce and William would be squealing and jumping up and down.

James prepared to take the wide-eyed marine corporals on another training exercise, but felt it was too cloudy to complete a helicopter training.

"This is your last one, isn't it, Sergeant?" asked Corporal Rodriguez.

Smiling, James said, "Yes, it is. Two more weeks to go and I'll be home with my boys." Everything in him wanted to cancel the training due to the cloudiness, but it wasn't his call. He decided to just shorten the training but went through with it.

"Let's get this baby up in the air." Within minutes, James's heart began to race, and he broke out in a sweat.

"First Sergeant, are you okay?" asked a young corporal.

"Just feeling a little queasy," he said. "You know that feeling that you get when something is wrong? Well, I got it." Just then, he saw a huge loom of smoke coming from the copter engine. There had been a malfunction causing it to spin out of control. It was heading straight into a low mountain. Seeing that a crash was inevitable, James kissed a picture of his sons. Closing his eyes, he whispered, "I'm sorry, boys." Neither James Cook nor any of the crew survived the fiery crash.

The boys had lost both parents within six months of each other, and everyone felt numb and confused. It was a beautiful service, but Regina wondered what she would do with the two toddlers. She wept as she held the folded-up American flag in her hands. "I was only expecting to keep the boys for six months then move on with my life. I'm not their mother," she cried.

Pastor Storm hugged Regina and said, "He knew that you were a good choice of a caretaker." The truth was that she always wanted to have her own children but never connected with the right man. Being a successful real estate agent had demanded most of her time. On the night of their father's funeral, she said, "Well, I guess I'll never meet Mr. Right, but that's okay. I've got you two boys to keep me company."

The death of James had been a sudden and unexpected loss. Pastor Storm and his wife had been a strong support system for James and Carolyn. Now they were a strong system for Regina. They even offered to keep the boys on most weekends for as long as Regina needed it. Mary Storm and Regina became great friends due to both caring for the twins.

Regina had met Mr. Alex Musick, a handsome stranger, at the supermarket about four months after James died. Both seemed to have much in common and seemed to want the same things in life. He was handsome and well spoken but was also a swindler of several wealthy single women. However, Mr. Musick didn't disclose to Regina that he was recently released from prison after a fifteen-year stay.

"Baby, I know we've only known each other for a few months, but I know all that I need to know," said Alex, kissing Regina's neck. The Storms had the twins for the weekend, and Alex had Regina all to himself. "How would you like to be Mrs. Musick?"

"Yes, I would love to marry you!" she screamed with excitement. Alex pulled out a beautiful ring and placed it on her finger. He failed to disclose that the ring was stolen from the last woman that he had lived with. "Oh my goodness. The boys are going to be so happy to have a man in the house." Regina had overlooked the fact that he had expressed no desire to meet William or Royce. "Now, you can finally get to spend time with the boys and hopefully form a strong bond."

Alex began kissing her while she was still talking. He looked at her and said, "Baby, that's a real shame about the kids losing their parents." He hesitated for a minute but then said, "The only thing is that I don't want no other man's kids. Besides, they aren't even yours. We can have our own kids."

For the rest of the night she tried to reason with him, but Alex told her that she would need to choose between him and the boys. "I'll think about it, okay?" she said. Although he was offended, Alex told her that he would give her a few days or he would have to move on. Regina was indeed smart, lovely, successful; but she also had a void that the toddlers could not fill.

Sunday couldn't seem to come fast enough for Regina to talk to Mary Storm. "Mary, guess what? I've met a wonderful man," said Regina, pulling Mary to the side. Mary wanted to feel excited, but she couldn't explain the uneasy feeling deep inside her gut.

"Well, how do the boys feel about him?" asked Mary.

"Well, he's never met the boys, but I am working on that. But he wants to get married. I know he will learn to love them as much as I do. He just kind of mentioned that he didn't want children, but you know, I think I can change his mind," said Regina.

"Honey, if he told you he didn't want children, that's probably what he meant. Have you prayed about it, Regina?" It was obvious that Regina was in love with Mr. Musick and there was no changing her mind. No prayer would change the stars in her eyes. Mary Storm prayed that everything would be all right. Being a pastor's wife, she had seen this same scenario before. She had seen the beginning, the middle, and the end of these situations. Regina was a strong yet lonely woman.

Due to Regina's work schedule, she usually didn't attend midweek service. Pastor Storm and Mary were happy to see her and the boys show up at church that night.

"Go give Mrs. Mary a hug," said Regina to the boys. William and Royce ran to give the Storms hugs and kisses. "Mary, could you please find a snack for the boys back in the church kitchen? I left home in a hurry and forgot to pack their snacks."

Mary told them to sit on the front row and she'd be right back.

"Royce, wait right here. I'll be right back," said Regina, handing him a sippy cup. Looking around, she snatched William by his hand and placed him in her car, then drove off. It took several minutes for the

Storms to realize that Regina had taken William and left Royce at the church.

"I can't believe she did this," cried Mary to her husband. Actually, Pastor Storm couldn't believe it either. The boys had been through so much already, and now, Royce was all alone. The toddler cried and searched for William every day inside the house. About eight months later, Royce stopped looking outside, under the bed, and in the closet. It took a while, but William's memory finally faded in young Royce's mind.

A year had passed, and usually Mary checked the mail, but one day she became ill. Pastor Storm checked the mail instead. To his surprise, there was a letter from Regina addressed to Mary Storm: "Mary, I am so sorry for what happened. I was so stupid and selfish. That man left me and took all my money. I still have William and plan to keep him with me. I just got married to a wonderful man and he plans to adopt William. Please don't try to find us because I can never come back again."

Reverend Storm quickly tore up the letter and never told his wife about it. He decided that as long as Royce had moved on from the pain and grief that he suffered, he decided not to refresh his memory. Reverend Storm decided not to talk about William, Carolyn, or James Cook to Royce. The child was loved and eventually adopted by this family.

Not only that but against his wife's wishes, he burned all the letters that Carolyn had written to Royce and William. They would never discuss any of Royce's past and hoped that he wouldn't ask any questions about it in the future. "If he asks, we'll just say we adopted him out of love, and that's all he'll need to know," said Reverend Storm.

"Okay, I think that's okay. We don't need to say anything more at this point," agreed Mary.

The Storms became terribly ill after a mission trip, on Royce's seventh birthday. Both of them were hospitalized for several months, and tragically, Royce Storm was placed into foster care. After it was discovered that he suffered physical abuse by his foster parents, the

Storms worked hard to get him back. "I love you, and I will make sure you'll have everything you'll need," said Pastor Storm to young Royce. With much love, patience, and understanding, Royce grew into a respectful and handsome young man.

Chapter 2

February Trouble

The years had dimmed Royce's memory, but since becoming engaged to Secret Bell, he had begun having flashes about his past. He didn't remember going to his own father's funeral. So much of his memory had been blocked. He couldn't remember his mother's face, but he did remember her hazel eyes. What happened to his father? Nothing made sense. He was an only child. Wasn't he? "Oh well, I was adopted by a good family," he would say every time a foggy memory would come up. Pastor Storm never discussed the details of Royce's adoption. All he knew was that he was in foster care for a short while, until some kind of paperwork was finished.

In the last few months, the foggy memories were becoming more clear, precise, strong, and even aggressive. Royce kept having a recurring nightmare that made him feel uneasy. It almost seemed as if a force wanted him to know something.

Royce was thrilled as he had hiked up an almost impossible green mountain. "Yes, I did it!" he yelled with his arms raised into the air. A wide grin came across the climber's face as he entered a beautiful rich emerald-green rain forest. Royce noticed that the forest was filled with gigantic sharp thorns on one side and beautiful plushy green grass on the other side. *I've got to climb this hurdle*, he thought. Although he was not a runner, Royce ran and jumped over a larger hurdle onto the green grass. Suddenly rich black oil came gushing out of the ground that he was standing on. He felt safe as he stood on the rich oily green grass.

The clear blue sky suddenly turned dark as thick storm clouds rolled in. Out of nowhere came a loud flashing fire truck with blaring sirens. Then a booming voice yelled out, "Look up!" A large mirror fell from the sky. He grabbed it and gazed into his own eyes. Startled, he looked up and saw the word "trouble" spelled out in the dark clouds. "Oh, Lord, what is that?" Before he could focus on that, he heard loud screeching wheels behind him. Royce watched in horror when out of the smoke limped a small dark figure with both hands stretched toward him. "No, get away!" Royce yelled so loud that he woke himself up. *Oh, man, another bad dream. What does it mean?* he asked himself.

Royce was becoming stronger in his faith in Christ. Studying the Scriptures, he read of many times that God spoke to his people through dreams. Was God trying to get a message to him? If so, what was it? Why now? Royce couldn't understand why he had peace about his past all these years, and now, all these memories were surfacing. He had dealt with his past, hadn't he? He had moved on, hadn't he? So many questions caused an unending frustration due to the timing. He was finally getting married to the woman he loved. Everything was good, wasn't it?

He was still thinking of who his best men would be. His closest friend lived thousands of miles away, in Germany. Davis Patton was his best friend and Marine pen pal. Davis was stationed in Germany ever since he joined right out of high school. After Royce's adoptive father's funeral, he found a letter from Master Sergeant Davis Patton. Royce didn't even know that his father had been writing different soldiers overseas and sending them care packages. Although most had been stationed elsewhere, there was one soldier who kept up with Reverend Storm. Royce happened to find several letters that Davis had written his father months earlier. "What kind of name is Davis? Two first names?" whispered Royce while looking at the envelope. It was sad, but Royce wrote him back and informed him that his father had passed. He expected that to be all, but instead, he received a letter back. Ever since that day, they wrote each other back and forth for years. Although they had never exchanged a picture, they told each other everything about their lives. Davis's mother raised him, but he joined the military after she passed away. He had a stepfather, but they were not very close. There were no other siblings for him to write or keep in contact with. Both were glad to have another man to talk to.

"Hey, man, can you send me a picture of Secret? I'd love to see what she looks like," asked Davis in a letter.

Royce responded with a definite "No way, man. I haven't even sent you a picture of me, so you know you ain't getting a picture of her. But trust me, she is beautiful." Davis asked if she had a sister. Royce shook his head and smiled while reading the letter. "Nope. You got to find love on your own, my brother," he wrote. Davis thought that was funny and drew a laughing face.

The soldier was glad to hear about Royce finding love. Although they were worlds apart, they had walked each other through so many trials. Writing kept the soldier calm and connected to someone in the States. He heard about how they met and the whole saga that happened last year. "I still can't believe that your baby's momma tried to sell your baby. Man, then your girl jumped in like Wonder Woman and gave her the what for. I hate I missed that chick fight!" said Davis in a letter. Royce's letters gave him something to look forward to, and he was up to date on all things Royce and Secret. He was actually being discharged later in the summer and was excited about attending his friend's wedding. With the life of a soldier, he just hoped that he would be alive to come back at all.

Picket Jones lay in solitary confinement at the Jefferson County Jail. Almost a year had passed since that first mug shot was taken. Her light skin and long curly hair reminded people of the late great actress Lena Horne. Actually some of her old drug buddies called her Broke Lena. Before drugs, she was intelligent and "drop-dead gorgeous." You wouldn't know it, but she even graduated at the top of her high school.

The day she was arrested was the absolute best and worst day of her life. It was obvious that Picket Jones was drunk and coming down from a crack cocaine high. Her body's need for drugs took her to the darkest place that she had ever been. Out of all of her illegal dealings, trying to sell her own baby for drugs led to her arrest. Picket was placed on suicide watch as soon as she was booked into the county jail. "I can't believe what I did! I'm going to kill myself. My baby . . . what did I do . . . ," she cried in the police car. Although her fight with Secret Bell had been over, it was as if Picket was still in a pitiful rage in the patrol car.

"Lady, stop it! Stop kicking back there, right now!" shouted the arresting Officer. The handcuffed lady had a black eye; but she kicked the seats, cursed, and then cried uncontrollably. Picket had to admit that she was an absolute mess. The jail officers could all see that her thin shaking frame had been ravished by her lifestyle of addiction.

"Do you have a religious preference?" asked the booking officer.

"Well, if I did, I probably wouldn't be here now, would I, honey?" said Picket. She was obviously high, but she later remembered that particular question. "I need to talk to the chaplain!" yelled Picket through her jail bars. It seemed that no one was listening to her, so she began to shout even louder. "Hey, I need to talk to the chaplain! I know ya'll got one! All the jails do!" she yelled. In frustration, the guard said, "He's on vacation, and he'll be back when he gets back." The officers came by every fifteen minutes just to make sure she had not harmed herself.

"Psssttt . . . I'm still alive, shorty," said Picket to an officer. "You took my shoestrings and eating utensils. Ya'll know I need, Jesus." She laughed loudly.

A guard yelled back, "Girl, you need somebody!"

Picket threatened to start acting up if they didn't get her someone to speak with, soon. It may have been jailhouse religion that she was after, but it didn't matter. Finally, she began to visit the chaplain, Reverend Johnny Black, nearly every day while she was there.

"I heard you wanted to talk with me, young lady," he said while speaking with her through the jail bars.

"Yes, sir, I messed up so bad. Man, I don't even know where to start," she cried.

"Well, Ms. Jones, I find it better to just start at the beginning."

Picket knew she wasn't going anywhere for a while, so she just let it all out.

Over the next few months, the guards, chaplain, and other inmates noticed a remarkable positive change in Picket. It was an involuntary soberness; her drug addiction had escaped her months ago. Picket realized that every wrong decision she had made was the result of her years of drug abuse. After many conversations with her spiritual advisor, Picket had given her life to Christ and received forgiveness for her sins. Being locked up helped her head get clear from the drug fog that controlled her life. The downside of being drug free was that she did have to think about her past decisions and mistakes. Over the past four years she had robbed people, lied to loved ones, and even sold her own body for drugs. Her tormented mind was clear enough to remember the thing that led her to use drugs in the first place. After reading so many books in jail, Picket realized that she had to get to the root of her addiction. Yes, it was going to be painful to revisit, but she had to make peace with her past.

Picket had been to several rehabs with her baby, Mercy Storm, several times. Within herself, she wanted to be clean and free from her raging drug addiction. "This time, Momma is going to kick it. I'm doing this for you, Mercy. I'm going to be a good mother," she would say to her smiling baby. For some reason, this broken mother would cry almost every time she looked into her smiling baby's eyes.

However, Picket had gotten recent news that she was going to be released from jail. She had not been feeling well, but her outlook was strong.

"I put in a good word for you with the district attorney. I think some of your charges have been dropped because you did everything you were supposed to do in here," said Chaplain Black. "Besides, you have basically served all your sentence." He pulled up a chair to her cell. Looking into her eyes, he said, "The jail is so overcrowded that higher-ups are trying to decide who to let out. Whatever is going on out there is causing folks to come in here."

Picket shook her head. "Lord have mercy. People don't want to be where I've been."

She wasn't sure if it had something to do with her declining health, but she was chosen to be released. Actually, for the last few years she had ignored symptoms of yellowing eyes, not wanting to eat, fever, and feeling tired all the time. The symptoms would seemingly vanish, then she would resume using drugs and alcohol.

Either way she didn't care why she was being let go. To her it was an answered prayer.

"Your child endangerment charges were dropped, so I'll see what options you have," said her attorney, Ms. Lawson. She was actually guilty of endangering her baby, and there were even witnesses. However, she had completed her mandatory classes and gotten clean in jail.

"Jones, wake up, Jones," said the guard as she banged on Picket's jail cell. "You're getting out today. Where are you going? Do you have any family?"

Smacking her lips, Picket said, "No."

She had actually come from a wealthy Christian family but had chosen a lifestyle opposite of how she was raised. She was an only child whose parents had died while she was in jail. It was a great weight that she would carry for the rest of her life. "I would have done anything to stop that carjacking. They were always there for me, but I was locked up when they needed me the most," she cried. Her parents left her plenty of money, but her drug addiction had taken her away from all her money and good senses. Like many drug addicts, crisis overcame her on the road to success. Crack cocaine and a reckless lifestyle had severely damaged her physical appearance. Worse than that, her choices had destroyed her once-tender heart.

With both hands placed over her eyes, Picket started shaking and became inconsolable. Guilt tried to overtake her, but the chaplain came over to her cell and said, "Oh, Jones, it's gonna be all right. The thing about broken bridges is that they can always be repaired."

"All right, Jones, that's enough of that. You are making a new start today," the guard said. "What do you want to do now that you've got your life together?"

Wiping her eyes, she held her head up and said, "I want to get my daughter back and show her I can be a great mother." Picket didn't know if she could ever get Mercy back after what happened, but she was going to try. After collecting her things, she walked out of jail a free woman. Well, at least for now.

Upon leaving the jail, there was a taxicab waiting for her. "Are you Ms. Jones?" asked the driver.

"Yes, I am. Who are you?" asked Picket with a confused look on her face. The now-free woman hadn't called anyone to pick her up from the jail. She didn't have any living relatives as far as she knew of. It had been almost a year, and she didn't have anyone to even call.

"Ms. Lawson called me and asked me to pick you up and take you home," he said. Then he gave her a set of keys in her hand. Picket smiled as she recognized a set of keys that she hadn't seen in almost a year. They were the keys to her parents' home.

"I guess it's my home now," she whispered while kissing the red key.

The jail nurse, Veronica Spacey, walked over to the cab and said, "I'll call you with the test results as soon as I know something."

Due to being wrapped up in her own thoughts, the free woman barely responded, "Oh, okay." Picket Jones had one thing in mind, and that was getting her daughter back from her ex- boyfriend, Royce Storm.

"Picket, did you hear me? Your health is vital to you getting your daughter, okay?"

"Okay, okay, I'll be waiting, Ms. Spacey," said the lady in a hurry.

"Chaplain Black, will you keep Ms. Jones in your prayers? I don't have a good feeling about her test results. She is sicker than what she knows," said Nurse Veronica.

"Is that why she was released so soon?" asked the chaplain.

"Yes, I had to talk to the judge because . . ." Veronica told the chaplain that Picket's symptoms were common in people who had a terminal illness. She had tested Picket several times and didn't like what she saw. The next set of results had not come in yet; she suspected what they might reveal.

Picket Jones had settled in her beautiful well-kept home. The solid wood floors were surrounded by thick plush rugs. The pictures on the walls were filled with loved ones full of smiles. Picket was reminded that she had come from a beautiful wealthy family. Her old room was full of beauty pageant trophies, debate trophies, and all honor roll certificates. The five-bedroom brick home was fully furnished and clean as if she never left. Mr. and Mrs. Jones always prayed that their daughter would turn her life around.

"Well, I may as well get started on getting my daughter back," she said while opening the curtains. Picket made a list of all the things that she needed to do to get settled. First, she needed to go grocery shopping, then get a decent wardrobe. Opening her purse, she looked at a list of local drug recovery groups. *I definitely need to contact them as soon as possible.* Like a hand fitting in a glove, Picket felt like her old self again. She was encouraged that she was going to be the woman that God planned for her to be. She also found a phone book and turned to the page of family law attorneys. Picket smiled as she looked out in the garage and saw that her black Lincoln Navigator was still there. Cranking it up, she thought, *Dad, you were awesome. You kept it up for me, didn't you?* A single tear rolled down her cheek as her heart filled with gratitude toward her parents. *I think I'll pay Royce a visit in a few days,* Picket thought while warming up her car. She knew the visit would not be pleasant, but she hoped he would be able to see the change in her. Her only intention was to get her daughter back, and hopefully, he'd agree to turn her over without too much of a fight.

Chapter 3

Secret Struggles

It was nearly 3:00 a.m. when Secret Ruffins Bell finally arrived home from her twelve-hour shift. Tiptoeing in the living room, she smiled when she saw her baby on his grandmother's chest. Justice was spread out on his grandmother like a squirrel that had been run over by a car. Helen's recliner was leaned back as far as it would go. Grandmother and grandson both had their mouths open. *Looks like they wore each other out today.* She eased into her room and slid into her queen-sized bed.

As a physician's assistant, Secret practically did everything a doctor did, except get paid like one. However, her pay was still rather good compared to her peers. She even had distant thoughts of having her own private practice one day. "Have you considered going to medical school and becoming a doctor? You are too good not to keep going," said her supervising physician.

"I would, but where would I possibly find the time?" She had actually thought about it but placed it in the back of her mind. Secret had bigger fish to fry right now and had a wedding to plan.

Secret reflected on the past year that was filled with turmoil, laughter, and so much more. She was strong, beautiful, and very courageous. Very few people had learned how to turn their pain into power, but Secret was one of those who had. She had begun to use her pain as a stepping stone and not as a burial ground. Putting her hand over her mouth, Secret couldn't help but laugh out loud, as she thought of the moment that she met Royce Storm. He was rude, greasy, and unhealthy but had been there during the worst time in her life. Her sleep overwhelmed her as she smiled thinking about that same rude man.

The bright sunrays and loud chirping of blue birds woke her up the next morning. She rolled over and put her large plush pillow over her head. The stress of planning another wedding brought out several of her nervous habits. "Shoot, look at my nails." Secret had already started biting her nails due to the stress of getting married again. "If I don't get ahold of myself, I'm going to have man hands," she whispered, scolding herself. At least she did have some old coping skills that she used when stress tried to take over, such as writing. Writing letters helped her to refocus from all her inner turmoil.

She couldn't send emails or text to one particular cherished loved one. She found it very therapeutic to use a good old-fashioned paper and pen. Of course, the paper could not contain the words of sympathy held within her heart, but she wrote anyway.

"Dear Destiny, you are over three years old now. I bet you have gotten so big and so pretty. I imagine that you have big brown eyes and velvet brown skin. You looked like a living doll on the day that we said goodbye. Are you allowed to have an attitude in heaven? I bet you are giving your daddy some real attitude, up there. It's so hard to believe that you and your father are both in heaven. At least you have each other, and God gave me someone too." Secret knew that her heart had completely healed because she didn't cry thinking of her lost loved ones. They weren't lost at all because she knew exactly where they were. Destiny Bell and Joel Bell had been in her past, and both were in her future. A tear hit her paper, but not a tear of sadness. A spirit of peace flowed from her pen. She wiped her eyes and continued to finish her letter.

"Destiny, guess what? You have a little brother now. Girl, he is the tiniest thing, but he is full of fire! Yesterday, he had the nerve to demand that I give him juice. I told him that he couldn't have any juice. That stinker threw his bottle down on the floor, banged on his high chair, and yelled out, 'Juice!' Can you believe the nerve of him being all demanding? I was like, 'Oh no, you didn't, little sir.' I can't imagine where he got that from. He is a tiny one-year-old, and I hate that you couldn't meet him. He is so cute and a real handful. You know he was born a few months early, so he figures he's got to be tough. I bet you would have been a great big sister and gave him lots of kisses. Mommy has had so many changes in her life and even a lot of love. Can you believe that someone loves your mommy? Don't tell your daddy, because he would come and start some trouble down here! I love you, and I hope to write you soon. Love, Mommy."

Smiling, she folded the letter and sealed it with a kiss. She opened her window, taped her letter onto a big red balloon, and allowed the cool breeze to take it into the heavens. "Oh, I have to get ready," she said, still looking into the sky. She always tried to follow the balloon with her big brown eyes to see how far it would go. It was so hard to believe that she had so many changes in such a short amount of time. Secret had to live through the bitterness of her husband's murder. Before that, she had to deal with the sudden death of her unborn child. Before that, it was the recovery of molestation from her mother's boyfriend. Her life had never been normal and certainly not easygoing. It could only be described as turbulent. However, God had given a stable ship to weather every storm in her life.

Secret could have never imagined in a million years that she could ever love another man more than she had her late husband. Joel Bell had been such a powerful force in her life for so many years. They even shared a home, love, and a beautiful child. She still lived in the same house that they shared together. Although she had placed a for-sale sign in the yard, she really struggled to let the home that she loved go. There was no way her future husband wanted to live in the same house as her late husband. Royce didn't even like to visit her there, but he knew he had to.

Royce had a lot going for him this year, and it was the happiest time of his life. After selling his restaurant in Jefferson, Texas, he opened a new booming one in Tyler. East Texans loved a good country meal, and the ladies thought the restaurant owner was a piece of eye candy. Secret rolled her eyes every time she would come in and see the place nearly filled with all colors of women. "Why are there always a bunch of smiling women in here, Mr. Storm?"

Royce would just shrug his shoulders at his fiancée and give her a kiss on the cheek. "It's all yours, babe."

He was such a good chef that he had found time to publish his first cookbook named *The Secret Ingredient: Healthy Soulful Eating*. The book was a testimony of his weight loss due to diet and exercise. None of that would have happened without his beautiful fiancée, Secret Bell. Although he was proud of his new book, he seemed kind of shy about his newfound book fame.

His publisher wanted him to have a picture of himself shirtless. He would be wearing an apron, a chef's hat, and cowboy boots. "I'm only selling cookbooks and nothing else," he told his publisher. "Besides, I can't do that. I'm a Christian." However, he did settle for wearing a tight gray muscle shirt and a chef's hat.

For some reason, mostly women purchased his books. "This man is fine with those large hazel eyes." one woman said while she tightly held her new signed copy of his book. Royce's fiancée would roll her eyes but grin a little bit every time she saw a smiling woman looking at the book's back cover.

Secret's love seemed to grow stronger for Royce each day. She found it nearly impossible to keep her distance from him. Even when she was at work, he engulfed her mind and her thoughts. Smiles and laughter would surface as he ran across her mind. *That boy is so crazy*, she thought, chuckling as she remembered a soft kiss on her neck.

Her passion didn't realize that she wasn't married, yet. They had to literally step six feet apart due to a few heated interactions. "Have mercy, Lord! We have to wait. Why do we have to wait? Oh yes, we are saved."

Secret had to talk to herself on a daily basis. She found it difficult but necessary to be apart from the man she loved.

Royce and Secret had both agreed to wait until marriage. They had both rededicated their lives and bodies to Christ for his service. Sex before marriage was not in God's plan for their lives. The attraction was real, the passion was real, but their faith was real too. Both found each other extremely attractive, but setting up boundaries was necessary. Besides, they had a lot of decisions to make concerning their future plans as a family.

She was still undecided on how to move forward to deeply commit her new life with Royce Storm. Could she keep her job as a nurse in Dallas? Should she move to Tyler with Royce? "Secret, aren't you going to move in with your new husband?" asked her grandmother, during one of their many conversations.

"Of course she is going to move in with her husband," huffed Secret's mother. Secret cringed because she actually struggled with the thought of leaving her blossoming career in Dallas and moving to East Texas. Besides, her son, Justice, had the best physical therapists that worked with him on a daily basis. He was born two months premature, but he was making great strides in his therapy.

Secret and Justice had already arrived at her grandmothers' house. She had to text Royce the directions. Royce had finally agreed to meet the women that raised this powerful woman. Family and friends were so excited to hear of their engagement. It was so romantic and such a good story of how Secret and Royce fell in love. Their story had been the talk of the church that Secret attended as a child. It was just a few months into the New Year, and everyone was excited for the news of a wedding

Royce had driven down for a large family dinner at Secret's grandmother's house, in Dallas. He felt a bit nervous because he was meeting the rest of her family for the first time. They had all heard about his proposal on Christmas, and a few of them had been there to see it all. "Girl, that was a real love story if I ever seen it. The way he walked out there and gently brushed her hair back . . . Girl, I was like I sure wish I had that kind of proposal," said Monica, Secret's cousin to her mother.

Everyone gave a girlish grin as she acted out the love scene that she witnessed a few months ago. "Girl, if she would have said no, I sure would have said yes! That man is fine."

An elderly lady's voice could be heard coming from the kitchen. "All right now, settle down before I get a fan, a switch, and some blessed oil." It was Secret's grandmother trying to calm down her excited great-niece.

Secret had been looking out of the window from time to time. She knew it was nearly a two-hour drive from Tyler, Texas, to Dallas. Royce drove up in his new midnight-blue Ford F-250 truck while racing his engine. "Show-off," said Secret while walking out to meet him. Royce threw both of his hands up as if he were defending himself. "Hey, don't be trying to have no midlife crisis on me," she said. Royce loved screeching down the road and throwing his arm out the window. Secret would roll her eyes every time Royce would do that.

"Hey, babe, I see you are looking good. You are so beautiful, and our babies are going to be gorgeous."

Secret frowned and cleared her throat. "Man, I just had a baby, last year. For goodness' sake, let Momma rest." They both laughed because Royce had a toddler also. "Hey, if you can handle that epidural, you can have as many kids as you want to. I'd love to see that." She laughed, rubbing his stomach. Royce asked where Secret's mother was. "Why do you want to know where my mother is?"

"Because I don't want to give you a big passionate kiss in front of your mom." He laughed.

Although Helen and Secret had been living together, they still needed work on their relationship. They had a turbulent mother-daughter relationship and even had a physical fight in the past.

"I'm glad that you two are working on mending your relationship, though. Your mother is something else," said Royce upon getting out of the car. It was a work in progress, but much healing had been completed. Royce knew all about the strained relationship that they had for most of her life. He noticed a smirk on his fiancée's face. "What are you smiling about?"

Secret shook her head and said, "Man, you don't know the definition of something else, until you meet the rest of my family."

"Oh, Lord, I feel like I'm a steak on the family grill."

"Royce, I can't wait for you to meet my eighty-seven-year-old granny," Secret said. Granny Bell was known to others as Hattie Bell Ruffins. "She is my father's mother, but I'll tell you more about that later, though." Royce looked at Secret with somewhat of a surprised look because she rarely mentioned her father. "You think I've had some hard times. Man, her story puts my little crisis to shame."

"Am I in for a long story?" he asked with his eyebrows raised.

Secret shook her head back and forth, indicating that he was. "Let me tell you what Granny told me." Royce leaned against his truck as Secret took him back in time.

Chapter 4

The "Bell" of the Ball

Windell and Ora Taylor had a small farm in Conway, Arkansas. They had five daughters in which Hattie was the eldest. As the eldest child, Hattie had to work harder than the others. Ora's husband resented her and the girls because they were not boys. "What are these girls going to do, besides have a bunch of babies and stay in the kitchen!"

"Hattie is as good as any son you could have," said Ora to her hateful husband. She helped her parents pick the cotton, milk the cows, make soap, and kill the chickens for food. It was hard at times, but also enjoyable because she loved to help cook. Ora taught her daughter everything she knew and even trained her to take care of her sisters. Ora was so young herself when she became a mother, and at times, she and Hattie were more like sisters. They were only thirteen years apart.

"Times were different back then. Girls got married a lot younger than they do now," Hattie would say, reflecting on her past.

During Ora's last pregnancy, Hattie had to take over all the inside and outside chores. Windell refused to go get the doctor when it was time for the baby. Instead, he demanded that Hattie deliver the baby. She was twenty years old but had never delivered a baby before. Hattie quickly found an old medicine book that her mother kept around the house. With a sigh of relief, she delivered her baby sister MaryAnn.

Two weeks later, Ora was not able to shake the horrible outbreak of influenza. Twenty-year-old Hattie sat beside her mother's bedside and nursed her mother using the medicine book. "Mother is getting worse. Please let me go find a doctor," Hattie asked her father. He finally agreed to find a doctor, but by the time he finally made it, Ora's fever was at 105. She was dehydrated and delirious.

"Hattie, take care of your sisters. Don't let your daddy send them away. Please, don't let him give my baby away." Ora gulped while grabbing her daughter's hand. Ora Taylor died leaving five daughters at only thirty-three years old.

Everyone felt sorry for the family, especially a young mother leaving a baby behind. "She was so young," said the funeral goers, shaking their heads. "What's going to happen to the baby?" they asked. Several families wanted to take Baby MaryAnn, but Hattie refused to give her up. Unfortunately, Hattie's father was more than willing to let his cousin's family take her.

"You did what?" she screamed as her father told her he had given the baby away. "Never! Daddy, you know Momma did not want that." She cried as her father slapped her across the face.

"I'll do whatever I want with the baby! I just wish I had somebody to take you."

Her father seemed anxious to get rid of the baby that he never wanted. As a matter of fact, he didn't want any of them. Windell went out and got drunk the night before his cousins were coming to get the baby. He slept for so long that the younger sisters thought he had died in the bed. Hattie heard someone coming down the road. Looking outside, she grabbed her father's double-barrel shotgun.

"I'm here to get MaryAnn," said Windell's distant cousin. He and his wife began opening the car door holding a baby blanket.

"Take another step and I will blow you away, Cousin!" she yelled. "If I were you, I'd get right back in that car. You will not take my sister, anywhere." Of course, they left and never came back. When her father awoke and objected, Hattie pulled out the shotgun and threatened to blow him away if he tried that again. He had a horrible hangover and shoved her out of the room. Neither of them ever mentioned it again. From that point, Hattie became the sole caretaker of her sisters. None of the girls cried when Windell died a few years later. It was suspected that he drank himself to death.

The Taylor girls all grew to be beautiful young women, with the guidance of their eldest sister. They fought among themselves like most sisters, including fist fighting, name-calling, and hair pulling. When they all had an unusually dreadful day, Hattie would make them dance to popular songs. Then they would laugh and form a dancing line with each other.

It could be said that hot tempers ran in the family, except Jean. Jean was naturally quiet, calm, and was a peacemaker. Everyone, including Hattie, told her the secrets that they held. Mae was Hattie's slightly younger sister. She was next in line after Hattie. Although she wasn't the eldest, she was very disciplined and could be described as the lawgiver. Mae would give the spankings to Jean, Lee, and MaryAnn if Hattie left her in charge. Nobody bothered Jean because she knew too many secrets. Hattie and Mae worked together like a well-oiled machine.

On normal days, Hattie would cook and provide discipline if needed. Mae, being a handy girl, was usually outside mowing the lawn, taking out the trash, or fixing things around the house. The other three were left to tend to themselves. While unattended, Lee beat up her sister over a pair of blue jeans. As Lee took a victory lap, Jean snuck up behind her and cut off her entire ponytail. As you can imagine, the fists, name-calling, and rolling around began. Mae intervened and beat them both up.

Hattie worked hard as a car factory worker, a lamp factory worker, and even a secretary. She was beautiful but rarely found love on a long-term basis. She never longed to be married or have children like other women in her generation. Raising her four sisters instilled a sense of loyalty in her and them. "We owe her everything," said Lee to Jean on several occasions.

Hattie had been so strong, so tough, and so unbreakable all her life. However, none of her sisters had managed to bring out her vulnerable side. Well, no one had, except Mr. James Ruffins who was just a stranger in Conway. He had stopped by the farm one day to ask for some water. "I can do all sorts of yard work and cooking too," said the kind stranger to a weary Hattie. The yard had been looking badly because the girls were going to school and Hattie worked during the day. He was handsome, and his smile was very deceptive.

Mr. Ruffins swept her off her feet, and after a short courtship, they married. All of the sisters still lived at home, so he agreed to move in and help Hattie take care of them. She was able to help him get a job at the Ford factory. James was sometimes calm on the outside, but inside he was ready to explode in fierce anger. Hattie was so happy after giving birth to her first child, Lamont. She never wanted to be a mother nor a wife, but her heart filled with joy upon seeing her beautiful son.

"I don't want you to have any more children, Hattie," said James after losing his job at the Ford car factory.

"I totally agree. I think one is all we can afford," she responded. Besides, her sisters still needed her attention. To James's dismay, Hattie became pregnant about five months after Lamont was born. Alcohol and other women became his escape after discovering that jobs were hard to come by. Since he had no outside job, James would help Mae do all the yard work, cook for the girls, and fix important things around the house. He seemed to be a big help, but inside he had other motives.

One summer day, James asked if he could help Mae change the oil in Hattie's car. She declined his help because he reeked of alcohol. "Have you been drinking, James?" asked Mae.

"Maybe just a little, but I do have a little in my pocket, if you want some," he said. She told him that she didn't want any and told him to go inside the house. "But you need my help, and you know you want a drink. You are old enough, aren't you?" James grabbed Mae by her waist and pulled her close to himself. "You're old enough for a lot of things, aren't you?"

"No, I don't want any alcohol, and I don't want you. Get away from me!" she said, trying to free herself from his powerful grip. James tried to force a kiss on Mae and grumbled about Hattie being pregnant again. "Get your hands off me, James!" James had become more forceful, and Mae could see that James's intentions had turned wicked in nature.

No one knew that James Ruffins had forced himself on other young women in several states. Looking into his eyes, Mae no longer saw her brother-in-law; his blank stare indicated that she was in a situation that she could not control. James became so enraged that he punched Mae upside the head and then choked her until she passed out. Looking around to see if anyone had seen him, he dragged her lifeless body inside the car.

Jean hummed a tune as she walked to the mailbox. She turned her face to Hattie's car because she heard the car door slamming. After, she ran inside the house to get Hattie's double-barrel shotgun. Jean quietly walked up to the car, creaked open the door, and placed the gun to the back of James's skull. "Let her go and I mean now," said Jean while gritting her teeth. "Whatever you are doing, you ain't doing it today. Not here and not with my sister."

Mae awoke and staggered to the house holding her throat. Due to Jean watching her sister stagger inside the house, James snatched the gun from Jean and emptied all the bullets out. "If you tell Hattie, I will kill you and all your sisters."

Jean looked at him with a fearless glare. "You don't scare me at all. You need to leave us alone and I mean now."

Calmly James sat down and began quietly whittling wood with his knife. "You know, Jean, everyone thinks you are so quiet, but I know the truth. From one killer to another, I can see that look in your eyes. You wanted to kill me, didn't you, honey?" he asked smugly. Jean didn't know what to say, so she just walked off.

No one understood why Mae left and joined the army the very next day, except Jean. Part of her felt happy that she would see the world, but there was a rage at what had almost happened to her sister.

Everything seemed to flow smoothly at the house, even with Mae gone. James continued to fix things around the house but avoided Jean at all costs. James was sitting at the table one evening drinking vodka and gin.

"James, I don't want you drinking around the girls," Hattie said.

"Shut up! This is my house, and I'll do what I want!" he screamed because Hattie reminded him that the house belonged to her.

"Lower your voice so you don't scare Baby Lamont."

"I don't care about that stupid baby. I don't care about your sisters. I can't find a job, and I want out of here."

That dormant temper flared out of Hattie like a volcano. "Oh, well, you haven't been a joy to live with yourself. Go on and get out of here!" she yelled, pointing to the door. "Mae would be home soon on leave anyway." Without warning, James slapped Hattie across the face and knocked her eight-month-pregnant body to the ground. Rubbing her face, she said, "I can't believe that you just did that. I thought you loved me. Boy, if I weren't pregnant, I'd . . ." She scuffled to get off the floor.

Everything was quiet the next day. MaryAnn, Jean, and Lee were all at school. Hattie hummed as she cleaned up the kitchen and folded the girls' clothes. It was getting close to Lee's prom, and Hattie had saved up to buy her a beautiful dress. *Lord, Jean is going to be cutting a rug in that dress*, she gleefully thought to herself.

Although her back was turned, Hattie heard James swing the screen door open. "Please be quiet. You are going to wake the baby." Just then, Baby Lamont awoke squalling. Hattie scolded her husband as he made a loud entrance. He had been out drinking with some friends and had been gone all night.

"Woman, don't shush me. This is my house!" he yelled. Rolling her eyes, Hattie walked toward the room to console the teething baby. She made it a few steps when James grabbed her by the throat and backed her out the door as forceful as he could.

"James, what are you doing?" she gasped. She looked into her husband's eyes, and all she saw was rage.

"I told you no more children. I'm going to make sure you don't have any more." With those seething words, he gave a violent push off the porch. Hattie landed first on her stomach and then fell on her side. The man she fell in love with and married had no regard for her life or the baby that she carried. There was no 911 back then, no cell phones, and no close neighbors. Hattie lay there bleeding for hours. She went in and out of consciousness due to searing pain all over her body. She could hear Baby Lamont crying inside the house, but she was helpless to do anything about it.

"Please, help me, James," she weakly asked as she saw his boots stagger by her body. No doctor had to tell her that the baby had died. "I felt life leave my body," she said many years later. Finally, her sisters came home and went for help. Hattie never saw her husband again.

Royce just looked at the road as Secret told him the story of her granny and all she suffered as a young woman.

"That woman is tough as nails, ain't she? Can you even imagine that, Royce?"

"No, babe, I can't," he said while grabbing her hand.

Secret's grandmother and all her sisters were elderly now and had survived many trials in life. "Granny Bell is stern and says exactly what she thinks. You just have to deal with it. She is a holy roller now, so she says, 'Honey, whatever happened is under the blood of Jesus,'" said Secret.

Each of her great-aunts had played a key role in her life. They each took a large part in her upbringing and young adulthood. "So what happened to the sisters once they left, Hattie?" asked Royce.

"Aunt Lee married into money. She even paid for most of my college, rent, and made sure I had the finest clothes. Aunt Mae was tough on me and kept me in line. She always told me that I would come up missing if I didn't straighten up. She scared me to death with her soldier's stare."

Royce was taking mental notes as Secret talked. He wanted to make sure to get on their good side. "Aunt Jean is still quiet, but when she talks, everyone listens. Finally, there is the baby, Aunt MaryAnn, who was a model back in the day. The funny thing is that she is still a diva at her age. That's where I got my style from. She made sure I had every hair in place, skin shining, and clothes matching to a tee."

Secret continued giving the lowdown on her great-aunts. "Well, they all moved in together after their husbands died."

"Good lord, what is this, an old lady book club meeting?"

"Shut up, don't be talking about my family like that." She laughed.

"Let me tell you one more funny story," said Secret to Royce. She was on a roll and obviously enjoyed talking about her grandmother. "You can imagine how mortified my mother, Helen, was when this happened."

Royce was reminded that Hattie Bell's son was Secret's father. "So that would make Helen her daughter-in-law?" asked Royce.

"Yes, and although Mom is Granny's daughter-in-law, she still calls her Mom, and they celebrate every Mother's Day together."

Royce could picture the story as Secret told him of what happened. He snickered as his fiancée flailed her arms and laughed. One year, they went to celebrate at a new restaurant in town. Helen thought they were going to have a fun time until Hattie's face turned downward. The old lady was known for showing out from time to time. Out of the blue Hattie yelled out, "Son, who's cooking back there?"

"Mother, don't show out," whispered Helen in a low but firm tone.

"Hush your mouth, girl. Hey, Chef, come on out here," she demanded. Helen could have slid under the table but frowned and crossed her arms instead. You could not tell that they were not related by the looks of it. One would imagine a teenage daughter being completely embarrassed by her mother. Hattie Bell had a way of making everyone feel uncomfortable at times. Others had to admit that she only said what other people were really thinking. "Who is back there cooking? Come on out here and let me see." If Helen could have created a hole in the floor, she definitely would have.

Clearing her throat, Helen whispered, "Mom, you are making a scene," while wiping her mouth with a thick white napkin. Everyone noticed the commotion that the old lady was making.

Without hesitation, the cook walked hurriedly out of the kitchen all while trying to hush her. "Ma'am, is there a problem?" he asked while looking around the restaurant.

Granny Bell looked the young man up and down and then shook her head. "Lawd have mercy, you're just a baby. You don't know what you're doing back there."

The poor cook was a slender red-headed, freckle-faced Caucasian man. He couldn't have been older than twenty-one. He held his head down, appearing somewhat embarrassed. Instead of becoming insulted, the young man shrugged his shoulders and said, "Well, ma'am, I'm doing the best I can. Our longtime cook quit a few days ago. I'm drowning back there."

"Child, shut your mouth."

He looked confused by her comment. "Ma'am, did you just tell me to shut up?"

She shook her head and said, "Hmmm, yes, child, I sure did." She started rambling inside her large brown purse.

"Mom, what in the world are you looking for in there?" asked Helen. Putting her purse down, Granny Bell asked the young cook to help her up from her chair. Hattie pulled out a large bottle of her own special seasoning. "Lord Jesus, Mom, where are you going? Sit down, right now."

Swatting at Helen, Hattie said, "Girl, mind your own business."

The old lady and the cook walked to the kitchen. No one said anything, but they all wondered what in the world was going on. Some laughed into their napkin. No one had seen a spectacle like that. Helen yelled out, "What are y'all looking at me for? I can't do nothing about it," as she wiped her mouth and threw down her napkin. Needless to say, Granny hired herself for the rest of the day, but the food was delicious. Although it was highly irregular, the manager didn't try to stop her because the food was so good. There were absolutely no complaints from any customer, and everyone ate good that day. The entire family and the community knew that Hattie Bell was serious about her cooking. "You better be glad the health department didn't come in here today," said the manager. Hattie told him that they would have been shut down for bad cooking if they would have showed up before she got into the kitchen.

Secret had many tales of her grandmother's high jinks. Granny Bell was funny, serious, strong, and full of life.

Chapter 5

Coffee and Kleenex

Everyone was taking turns peeking outside looking at the engaged couple. "When are they coming in?" asked Lee. Mae told her that Secret was probably giving him the lowdown on the family.

"Leave those young folks alone," said Hattie to her nosey sisters.

"Royce, can we sit in the truck for just a few more minutes? I want to tell you a little more about my family history."

Royce felt as if he were being pulled through a portal of thirty years ago. Secret watched as Royce propped his seat back and folded both arms behind his head. "This seems like this is going to be quite a story," he said while reaching for her hand. It was not a pretty story. It was not a sugarcoated version of life. Calamity had struck this family, and the truth was raw and uncut.

Secret took Royce back about thirty years to begin telling the story.

It was a clear and beautiful day. As usual, Hattie went to see her only son, Lamont; his wife, Helen; and their two toddlers, Secret and Sweetie. She received news about some kind of minerals being found on her family's land back home.

"Lamont, guess what? I got good news from back home!" said Hattie, walking up to the door. The house was full of law enforcement and ambulance trucks. What was going on?

Two-year-old Secret sat there still playing in her playpen. Helen noticed that her hair and clothes were soaking wet. The toddler looked around the room due to all the excitement that was going on.

"Lamont, what is going on here? Lamont!" shouted his mother.

An officer stopped her as she walked through the living room. "Madam, this is a crime scene. You can't go in there."

"Crime scene? What? Son, what is going on?"

The mental health officer met Hattie as she attempted to keep walking through the house. "Ms. Hattie, my name is Officer Night, and I have been talking to your daughter-in-law." She pointed toward the restroom.

"Where is my son?"

Officer Night just kept talking about Helen. "I finally convinced her to drop the knife that she stabbed your son with."

Hattie leaned back and nearly lost her balance. "Stabbing? Knife, what is going on?"

Helen could be seen sitting on the side of the bathtub with her hands over her eyes. Due to all the blood on her hands and clothes and her desire to die, the officers decided to place Helen in handcuffs. As she looked at her lifeless baby's body, she said, "Please tell my mother-in-law what happened, because I can't."

Officer Night informed Hattie on how her son had killed her other grandchild. Helen had to kill him to save another life. "She just snapped a little while ago. We had to talk her out of killing herself." It was one of the worst family killings that any of the officers had ever seen. Although she didn't cry, her heart ached for her daughter-in-law's obvious pain.

Hattie Bell grabbed two-year-old Secret and kissed her on the cheek. "Did she see anything?" asked Hattie to Officer Night.

She whispered, "Yes, she witnessed the murder of her sister, but that's not the worst part. Your son tried to drown her in the bathtub, but Helen stopped him."

"Oh, you poor baby." Hattie began to weep and kiss her granddaughter. "You're all I have left, baby."

As Helen was being led away in handcuffs, she tearfully whispered, "Ms. Hattie, could you take care of my baby girl? Will you make sure Sweetie has a good funeral?"

"No, I can't do that," said Hattie with a stunned look on her face. This woman had just killed her son, and by right she should have been outraged. But . . . how could she? Lamont had done a horrible thing, but his mother still loved him. She still grieved for a murderer because she once held him in her arms. Drugs had taken not only her son, but also her grandbaby.

Helen screamed out, "I don't have anyone else! My mother is dead! God, please help me!"

Hattie recognized that cry that only comes from a woman with a broken heart. Perhaps she and her daughter-in-law were more alike than she thought.

"Hey now, baby, you know I got you. I will take care of everything," Hattie said while choking back her own tears. She wanted to reach out and hug her, but Helen still had blood on her hands and her clothes.

That day, Secret lost her father, twin sister, and nearly her mother. "Oh, baby," said Hattie, leaning over to her grandbaby. "What are we going to do?" she sobbed. Secret raised her arms toward the lady who had kept her many times during her two years.

"Gwan, Gwan . . . Mommy . . . Sweetie," Secret babbled as she held Granny's face in both of her tiny hands.

"You tell Granny all about it, baby." They both seemed to be wiping each other's tears. Although her words were not plain, her heart sure knew pain. She could not express all the horror that her little eyes had just witnessed. Secret seemed to be trying to tell her grandmother everything that had happened. Of course, she didn't have the vocabulary to fully explain witnessing her twin sister's murder.

The officer allowed Hattie to take Secret home but told her that Child Services would be calling her soon. She packed a few clothes, put the baby in the car, and took her to her new temporary home. Helen promised to come and get her daughter as soon as she could. "When you are ready, just come and get her, okay?" said Hattie. Helen agreed to come as soon as she was discharged from the state mental facility. Helen was discharged after a few months in the hospital, but she did not return to pick up her child.

Baby Secret was so traumatized from her experience that she stopped talking for an entire year. "Poor baby keeps waking up screaming," Hattie told her sister on the phone. Secret was comforted each time her loving grandmother would hold her tight in her arms. "Come on, baby, let's dance." Secret would begin to smile as her grandmother would kiss her on her little neck and dance the electric slide. "Now that's better, pumpkin," whispered Hattie. Everyone gave up on little Secret except Granny Bell Ruffins.

She just kept right on talking to Secret about her plans for the day, her dinner choices, and her life experience. One day, Granny was asking three-year-old Secret if she wanted some fish for dinner. "Girl, I know you love fish, but do you want fried potatoes or greens?" Secret giggled as her grandmother leaned over and looked under the cabinet with her knee-high stockings on. The talking lady didn't expect Secret to say anything of course. Granny's mouth hung open as she heard, "Child, please."

Looking around, she asked, "Who said that?"

"Child, please, I want gweens," said Secret with a huge tearful grin.

Granny Bell let out a deep belly laugh as she took Secret in her arms and hugged her. "Girl, you are a mess, you little stinker." As if that wasn't shock enough, the little stinker began to sing her favorite song, "Twinkle, Twinkle, Little Star." "Well, I'll be . . . girl, and you can sing too. What have you been thinking all this time?"

Her grandmother was there for every step of Secret's recovery. Secret had a beautiful room at her grandmother's house, but she refused to sleep in it. She slept with her grandmother every night simply because "she wanted to." At first, she slept on her grandmother's chest every night for the first few years. "Baby, you are getting heavy. Granny needs to breathe, so you got to sleep in front of me, okay?" Four-year-old Secret didn't fully understand that she had been eating good Southern cooking. Those little thighs were putting on some weight. Hattie asked Secret if she wanted to sleep in her beautiful room.

"No," she replied as she snuggled up to her grandmother. Hattie figured out that she was in it for the long haul and this was her roommate until "God knows when."

Secret stayed with her grandmother for the next nine years. Her great-aunts also made sure Secret had whatever she needed. One day, unexpectedly, Helen came and picked up Secret and took her home.

"Well, that's how it was told to me," said Secret, shrugging her shoulders.

Royce felt sorry that the love of his life had suffered so much. "Man, y'all's family was really messed up."

Secret frowned. "Well, that's a weird response to a god-awful story."

Royce grabbed her ring finger and gently kissed it. "I think a big warm hug is in order, Ms. Ruffins Bell Future Storm," he said.

Secret smiled through her tears and said, "Mr. Storm, you'd better stop kissing my hand like that or a lot more than a hug may happen."

Royce returned the look. "Woman, I'm saved. Please leave me alone. I think a hug would be simply fine. You're not getting me in trouble with the Lord. I've done enough on my own."

With a faraway look in her eyes, she said, "I was just thinking about something. If it hadn't been for her, I would have lost my mind."

"What do you mean?"

This time Secret leaned her seat back and crossed both of her arms around her head. "Well, something awful happened to me the day that my little Destiny died. I already told you how crazy I was after I tore up the hospital room." Shaking his head, he recalled how she had told him about how her unborn baby died a few years ago. Secret continued, "When I came home, I locked myself in my bedroom for three days. My husband couldn't get me to come out, and I wouldn't let him in. He called everyone he could think of to come and get me out. He called my mom, cousins, and my friends, but I wouldn't open the door for anyone." Royce could see that Secret was sharing a very personal experience. Cuffing her hands softly across her lips, she painfully said, "I refused to cry, comb my hair, come out, eat, or shower. Being a nurse, I know about mental health, but I was powerless to stop myself from sinking into this huge black hole."

A single tear ran down Secret's cheek as she turned back to face her fiancé. She continued to speak as he wiped her tear away. "Finally, it was the day of Destiny's funeral, and I had no strength to unlock the door. He kept telling me that we had to bury the baby, but I couldn't even imagine such a thing. Then he picked up the phone and called the right person, my granny." Now hugging, Royce brushed his future wife's long hair as she smiled through her tears. "Granny came over with Starbucks coffee, sunglasses, and a box of Kleenex. She banged her walker on my door, and then she demanded that I let her in. She came in, sat on my bed, and said, 'Baby, do what you need to do. Get it out because Granny understands.'"

This testimonial was very emotional for Royce to hear. He felt sorry for all that the love of his life had suffered. Secret wiped her eyes with Kleenex as she told Royce that she tore up that room from wall to wall. She cried, screamed, tore all her clothes out of the closet, and tore the wallpaper off the walls. Granny Bell had sat there quietly sipping on her own cup of decaffeinated coffee. She seemed to be in complete peace while watching Secret unleash the pain of her loss. After the raging woman was completely exhausted, she collapsed into her grandmother's arms. With a faint grin, Secret said, "I know a mother's arms is special, but ain't nothing like grandmother's arms." Royce's eyes filled with tears. "Honey, she had to literally put my clothes on just like she did when I was a child. The only thing hanging in my closet was a yellow nightgown. So that's what she slipped over my head and pulled over my shaking shoulders. I was a mess, but I was there in a yellow nightgown and fluffy Tweety Bird house shoes. Holding me by both shoulders, Granny marched me out of the room while I sipped my coffee. She put my shades over my red eyes and wiped my runny nose."

Joel, Secret's husband at the time, had been so scared hearing all the noise and yelling in the room. Although he was usually in control, this was one time Secret's husband didn't know what to do or how to help his grieving wife.

"I bet you tore it up, didn't you, babe?" asked Royce, touching her shoulder.

Secret gave a tearful smile. "Man, you know I did. You see, I had to always be strong and in control without a hair out of place. But life threw me something that I couldn't handle. And you know, Joel had to fix it."

Royce laughed just thinking of him being in that same situation. He also found it funny that Secret could talk about her first husband, and he felt no jealous emotions.

She continued her story. "My granny and all her sisters were there holding me up." Secret laughed as she told Royce that the old ladies told her own husband, Joel, to stand back because they had it under control. He didn't argue because he was completely outnumbered. Royce smiled because he already felt outnumbered. "Well, I just wanted you to know how important she is to me," said Secret.

"I got it, babe," said Royce.

"I can't even describe how much of a support system she was to me when Joel died. It was just two years after my little Destiny died. I collapsed in her arms after I got the news of his murder. She came over to my house again and just said, 'There, there, baby, just do what you need to do.'" Secret gave a tearful grin. "Babe, she came with a vanilla latte, tissue, and sunglasses. I was already in counseling when Joel was killed. So you know I was in trouble," Secret said. She reviewed the whole crazy funeral and what transpired after that.

Royce listened very patiently. "Well, babe, I don't know if I should say this or not. You wouldn't have met me or Mercy if all that had not happened. God took your sadness and gave you joy. And by joy, yes, I am talking about myself," he said, smiling.

Secret just hugged Royce in response to his statement. He told her that he was ready to go in and "face the music."

Royce was not just marrying Secret Ruffins Bell, he was also marrying all those who were important in her life. Hattie was in her late eighties, but she could still burn in the kitchen. She even published her own cookbook several years previously, *Hattie's Country Cooking*. She smiled once she learned that her granddaughter was marrying a chef. The fact that he owned his own soul food restaurant made her super excited. Everyone had tried to get her recipe for her famous sweet potato pie and corn bread dressing for many years. Her dishes were "slap your momma good!" She told everyone that they would have to pry the recipe from her cold dead fingers. Hattie didn't play when it came to her food. She had told her granddaughter on several occasions that her food needed some help. No one needed to look far to see where Secret got her attitude from.

Hattie hoped to have a throw down with her future grandson-in-law in the kitchen one day. "New school is good, but ain't nothing like that old stick-to-your-bones cooking."

"Granny, please be good when we get there. You know how you are."

"Girl, hush your mouth. I know how to talk to people," said Hattie, smacking her lips. Secret wasn't concerned about her talking as much as her actions.

"Hello, everyone," said Royce, entering the room filled with old ladies.

"Come on in here with your fine chocolate self," said Aunt MaryAnn, hanging on his large muscular arm. Everyone had been looking out of the window anyway. The truth was that Secret had good taste in handsome men. "It's a pleasure to meet a real superstar," she said. Royce was a long way from being a superstar. He had sold a few thousand copies of his new book, and he was considered up and coming. "You look even better in person," said Aunt MaryAnn, smiling and looking upside his head.

Secret held her head down and thought, *Oh lord, here we go.*

These ladies were wrinkled with time, their hair was long and gray, but grace radiated from their brown skin. Royce couldn't help but notice how beautiful all Secret's family was. He had never seen so many beautiful elderly women in his life. He smiled knowing just what his future wife would look like in fifty years.

"You can sit by me, big boy," said Aunt MaryAnn, patting beside her. Royce noticed a beautiful teenager come out of the kitchen. He found it funny that the girl obviously looked just like her grandmother. She handed MaryAnn a hot cup of coffee. "Thank you, honey," she said, giving the young lady a kiss.

"Wow, your granddaughter is so pretty," Royce said to his admirer.

Everyone in the room fell out laughing as MaryAnn rolled her eyes. "Oh lord, this always comes up."

Looking around, Royce didn't know what everyone laughed about. Secret whispered to her confused fiancé, "That's her daughter, not her granddaughter."

"Say what?" he whispered.

From the kitchen, Granny Bell yelled out, "Yes, that menopause caught you, didn't it, Ann?"

"Shut up, Bell."

Secret told Royce that her aunt was forty-seven when she was caught in a surprise pregnancy. "I hope to God that doesn't happen to me," said Secret while shaking her head.

"Girl, hush. If you're still looking good at forty-seven, I don't know what may happen," joked Royce, caressing his fiancée's cheek.

"Don't play with me, sir. I'm saved, but I still have that stabbing spirit that I'm trying to get rid of."

Royce rolled his eyes but sat down with a huge boyish grin. Out of the kitchen slowly walked Granny Bell on her walker with baseballs on the end. "Hey, hey now, looking like a good big old steak," she said while grinning. "I heard you used to be heavy on those biscuits, son. You was a big old buggar bear." She laughed.

Royce cleared his throat. "Yes, ma'am, I was very overweight at one time."

"Son, I bet you were eating up a storm, weren't you?" asked Granny Bell. Royce just shook his head and grinned.

Royce whispered to Secret, "What's with all the name-calling, Big Boy and Brown Round?"

Secret grinned and rubbed his hand. "Just be glad Aunt MaryAnn hasn't rubbed her fingers through your hair. They just think you're big and handsome, that's all." He didn't know whether to feel uncomfortable or flattered by these old ladies.

Although Royce didn't see it, he was very handsome. Just then, Aunt MaryAnn came and rubbed her fingers through his hair. "What kind of hair oil is that, son? It smells like Jamaican castor oil and coconut."

"You guessed it. That's what it is." Royce looked at Secret, hoping to be rescued, but she just smiled with pure enjoyment. She was eating all this up. In the past, Royce had given her a tough time, but now he was getting payback from her family. They were out of her business and in someone else's.

Over the next hour, the ladies had many stories to tell about Secret. Aunt Mae said, "Son, did Secret tell you what happened her senior year in college?"

Shaking her head, Secret said, "Aunty Mae, I'm sure he doesn't want to hear these old stories."

"Oh, yes, I do!" he interrupted," while rubbing his hands together. "Let me tell it," said Hattie to Mae.

"Well, my grandbaby was dating some knucklehead at the time. He got mad and slapped my baby in the face. They had an argument, and I guess he lost his natural mind. My sisters and I were already headed that way to come and visit. When we drove up, all I heard was my baby hollering and screaming. Child, when that door swung open, that young man was skipping out of there with Secret hitting him in the back with two skillets." Secret just held her head down as her grandmother told the whole story.

"Was he skipping, Bell?" asked Aunt Mae to Granny Bell.

"Girl, you know he was skipping every time she hit him."

It was funny to see old ladies laugh. Just then, Secret interrupted, "Royce, when I told my granny and aunts that my boyfriend had slapped me in my face, Granny tripped him with her cane. He fell, and they all jumped on his behind."

Granny Bell said, "We sure did."

Royce knew that Secret was quick tempered and refused to be mistreated. After meeting her family, he didn't have to look far to see why she was so feisty.

"Secret, didn't we forget to bring in our food from the car?" asked Royce, motioning her to follow him outside.

"No, I don't think we did. Oh, what?" She had a surprised look on her face but read his cues. "Oh, yes, we left some stuff in the car. Granny, we'll be right back." she yelled toward the kitchen.

"Okay, y'all come on in here when you get back in," came a response from the kitchen.

Without a word being said, Secret patted Royce on the shoulder. The man obviously needed a break from his new family. "Are you okay?"

Royce told Secret that he just needed a breather. After all, he had no family except his daughter, and being with his future family brought up raw emotions. "I know y'all are crazy, but it still makes me miss the family that I never had," he said.

"Well, I will loan them to you and all the crazy that goes along with this bunch."

Smiling, he grabbed his love around the waist then pulled her back toward the house. "Let's get this grilling over with," said Royce with a faint smile.

Chapter 6

Countdown to Heaven

Granny Bell told everyone to gather around while the food was getting ready. "We were just about to sing and finish talking about my funeral." She was looking at Secret while she mentioned singing.

"What funeral?" asked Secret to her mother, Helen.

"Girl, your granny is planning her funeral while she is still alive."

"Granny, what is going on?" Secret asked, getting off the couch. Everyone in the room already knew what was going on. Granny Bell wanted to hear what everyone was going to say at her funeral while she was still alive. She wanted to see if her wishes would be carried out like she asked.

"Secret, I have just put on a fresh pot of coffee," said Granny Bell. Secret held her head down because she knew that her grandmother had some sort of bad news. Ever since Secret was a child, Granny would give her either hot chocolate or decaf coffee when there was bad news. Secret twisted her lips to the side as her grandmother poured her a fresh cup of coffee. "Baby girl, doesn't that smell good? I even have your favorite vanilla creamer."

Secret sipped her coffee slowly but looked at her granny all side-eyed. "Okay, Granny, spit it out."

"Baby girl, it's back." Secret knew what the dreaded "it" was. Hattie patted her granddaughter's hand and then took a sip of coffee. "The cancer has spread to my lungs, liver, and breast." Granny Bell had beat cancer once before, but this time it had returned with a vengeance, so she decided not to pursue any lifesaving treatments.

"But, Granny, you can beat it this time like you did last time. There are new experimental drugs available. At my hospital, we are trying out new things all the time. I will put your name on the list first thing Monday morning." Secret was talking so fast that she looked as if she were running out of breath.

Hattie gently put her wrinkled finger on Secret's lips as she frantically spoke. "No, baby girl, not this time," said Hattie, giving Secret a side tight hug. "I am going out the way that I want."

"No, Granny! You have to fight this. We can beat it this time."

"No, baby. Granny is not fighting anymore. I've already made my peace with God. Now, you have to accept that Granny can't fight anymore." Secret's eyes filled with so much water that she couldn't see. Her lip turned downward and quivered. She looked like a toddler that was about to have a squalling fit. Of course, Hattie had seen that same look hundreds of times. "No, baby, don't do it. Lakeshia, you've got to be strong for me."

"Okay." It took all the strength that she had just to get that "okay" out without choking on it. "How long did they give you, Granny?" asked Secret tearfully.

"They said I had about six to seven months, but only God knows for sure." Changing the subject, she asked, "Secret, don't you have a wedding to plan?"

"I know what you're doing, and it's not going to work this time." Secret let out a huge wail and bent down on the floor. She felt as if she had been hit with a seven-ton truck. "Granny, my heart just fell out of my chest," she sobbed.

Hattie took her granddaughter in her arms and just held her until she stopped weeping. "Okay, now, baby, let me ask that again. Don't you have a wedding to plan?"

Once again Secret felt as if she had to pick up her broken pieces. It was hard to get herself together, but she managed to answer, "Yes, I do." Royce had been looking wide eyed the whole time. He didn't know what to do or say. Part of him wanted to run away from all the drama going on in the kitchen. Since he was the fiancé, he figured he had to tough it out and be supportive of Secret.

"My lord, look at that ring. Simply beautiful," said Hattie while holding up Secret's hand.

Secret whined, "Granny, with everything going on, how can I even plan for it?" Now the streaming tears were in full effect; and Secret wailed, shook, and paced. Hattie was determined to get the attention off herself.

Royce thought, *Man, if Secret is taking it this hard now, I can't imagine how she is going to act at the actual funeral.*

"Baby, when is the wedding date?" Hattie asked.

Royce said, "December," and Secret said, "August." Both looked at each other and laughed. "Well, I guess we need to narrow that down," said Secret, blowing her nose. She felt that she had gotten all her crying out for the time being. "Granny, will you promise to hang on as long as you can?"

Hattie placed both of her wrinkled hands on each side of Secret's tear-stained cheeks. "Yes, I promise to be at your wedding whenever it is." She took her bony finger and tapped Royce on the nose. "But I'd advise you not to wait too long. I do have an appointment with Jesus, you know."

Turning toward Royce, Secret asked if they could have the wedding in August. He kissed her ring finger and said, "Of course."

Hattie smiled and shouted, "Beautiful hot August is a wonderful time to have a wedding in the South. We'll all sweat together. Secret, do you have a favorite flower for your wedding?"

"Granny, you know I love roses. I want roses everywhere," said Secret, smiling.

Royce and Secret both wanted a beautiful yet small ceremony with just friends and family. They would also find a perfect place to hold the wedding. Hattie placed her hand in her apron pocket and pulled out a blue envelope. "Son, don't open this until after your wedding, okay?"

"Yes, ma'am, Ms. Hattie." She didn't even know him. Why would she give him an envelope? What was in it? Then she whispered something in his ear that made him hold his head down. "Oh lord, . . . what . . . absolutely not . . . I can't," he whispered as she spoke into his ear.

"Granny, what are you asking my future husband? What are you asking him to do? He can't do it!" Waving her arms, Secret said in a low tone, "Royce, don't do it."

Hattie quickly changed the subject. "Baby, are you going to sing for Granny?"

"Uh, no, ma'am, I'm not," Secret snapped back. Granny then turned her attention to Royce. She was hoping to get some kind of support from him. He didn't even know that Secret could sing. "My baby stopped singing a long time ago. She had the voice of an angel." Turning her eyes toward the girl that she raised, she said, "Baby, I want to hear your voice before I die, okay?" Royce hadn't seen Secret struggle like that in a long time.

"Granny, I'm not sure that I can do it." She said that she would think about it, but she didn't want to.

The truth was that Secret did have the voice of an angel. Her voice had an unlimited range; it could go from a low alto to a high soprano flawlessly. She left people in tears even at the age of twelve. Unfortunately, life interrupted, and she was molested by her mother's boyfriend. Not only had an evil act stolen her innocence, but her voice went with it. It was like someone had thrown a wet heavy blanket on a warm, cozy fireplace. Young Secret was fiery, full of life, and had so much hope in her heart. Darkness had stolen her most precious gift, her voice. Not only had she cut off her long hair in a fit of rage, but she vowed that she would never sing again. Since no one was there to hear her screams, no one would be there to ever hear her song.

Springtime was fast approaching, and Royce and Secret were two peas in a pod. When Secret wasn't at the hospital working, she was in Tyler, Texas, at Royce's restaurant. He had moved the Secret Place Restaurant to Tyler, and it was doing quite well. His book sales drew people to his delicious food. Most of the people wanted to taste his healthy Southern recipes. However, a lot of women just wanted to see the author in person. He was quick to pull out his fiancée's picture and tell them that he was engaged to be married.

Mercy had her permanent spot in his office. Although she was too big for a playpen, she had a colorful play area in the corner. The two-year-old had plenty of toys, blocks, and dolls to keep her busy. The only thing that she didn't have was a great hairdresser.

"Royce, what in the world is wrong with that girl's hair? You know she's a black woman, don't you?" asked Secret, frowning while running her fingers through Mercy's hair.

"Woman, I'm doing the best that I can. You know that I'm not a beautician," said Royce as he shrugged his shoulders.

"Girl, you look a hot mess, and you don't even know it. You poor baby. Your daddy should be ashamed of himself." Mercy didn't know what her future stepmother was talking about. Secret couldn't wait to take care of her new stepdaughter on a regular basis. Mercy was happy, and she believed that her daddy was the king of her world. Although she couldn't tell him, she was proud of all that he had accomplished too.

"Let's go see your future daddy," said Secret to Justice while placing him in his car seat. Secret decided to drive to Tyler one day to see Royce. After driving from Dallas, they arrived at the Secret Place Restaurant. As usual, Baby Justice was looking around the room for Mercy.

"I know who you're looking for, little man," said Royce, giving the baby a big kiss. "Come on, man, give me five." Royce held up his hand and slapped it against Justice's. The truth was that Royce was not his biological father, but no one would know. They were very close, and their bond was very strong. Justice would laugh and giggle every time Royce would kiss him on his face and neck. Royce was on the list for the doctors, therapists, and daycare to call in case something happened to Secret. It was the same way with Mercy. Secret was on all the daycare contact forms as the first contact if Royce could not pick up his child. They were already a family; all that was needed was the official wedding ceremony.

Secret sat in his office looking at a wedding dress magazine. She became quickly annoyed due to Royce's phone ringing continuously. He kept looking at the number and pushing silent. "Who keeps calling you?" Baby Justice was playing with his soon-to-be sister in the corner. At first, Royce tried to ignore the curious female in the room. "Babe, who keeps calling your phone?" Royce tried to play it off by telling her it was a wrong number. "Boy, don't even start lying to me. Are you cheating on me?" she asked with her arms folded.

"Woman, I wouldn't have time to cheat if I wanted to," he grumbled while looking through some papers on his desk. Secret asked to see his phone. After he told her no, she snatched it from his hand. "Oh lord, here we go." This was not the first crazy woman that had ever been in his life. Royce held his head down as Secret's bucked eyes pierced through him. She couldn't believe who kept calling him. It was another woman calling her fiancé, but to her surprise, it was someone that she knew.

"Royce Storm, why is my granny calling you over and over? What is going on here?"

Shaking his head, he quietly said, "I can't tell you."

With a rolled neck and a rolling eye, she cleared her throat very loudly. "What? Why?" she asked.

"Because if I do, you are going to kill me. Matter of fact, the whole family is going to kill me. Granny made me promise that I wouldn't say nothing." Although Secret had a piercing stare, Royce stood firm and would not open his mouth.

"Well, be like that then. That's my granny, and ya'll better not be planning nothing stupid. Don't let my granny get you beat up by the rest of the family." Royce already knew that it was too late for that. His mind drifted as he imagined Granny Bell's sisters kicking his behind down the street on canes and walkers.

For someone dying, Granny Bell had to take what seemed like tons of medicine. "Why do I have to take all of this medicine?" asked Hattie at every medical visit.

"Ms. Hattie, we both know that you are not taking half of this medicine that I am giving you." Dr. Smith, her primary hospice care provider, knew that his dying patient could be very persistent. Nobody could make her do anything, not even give another round of chemo a try.

Once she was placed on hospice, Hattie was provided a personal care attendant. She became like one of the family. One day Granny Bell's worker, Shelia Ruth, had given her a shower, rubbed her feet, and given her all her medication. "Oh, baby, thank you. You take such good care of me," said Hattie in a real tender voice. "Could you get me some socks out of the back room?" Hattie had made a habit of spitting out her medicine when Shelia would turn her back. Besides, she wanted to be in her right mind when her soon-to-be grandson-in-law came. For a sick woman, she had plenty of fire left although she had a short life to live.

"Granny, are you sure you want to do this?" asked Royce while whispering on the phone. He held the phone away from his ear as Hattie gave him an earful. She went on and on about her limited time here on earth. She just needed him to do one thing. It was only four weeks after their first meeting, but Hattie knew he was the one for the job.

Finally, the day of their secret adventure had arrived. Secret had called Royce and told him that she had found a nice tuxedo for him. She was excited and anxious to show him what she found in her wedding magazine. Feeling nervous, Royce had made all kinds of excuses as to why Secret could not come to the restaurant that day. He told her that he was going out of town, which was true. He just didn't tell her what he was really doing while he was out of town.

"Shelia, I'm so tired. I really want to be left alone this afternoon," said Granny Bell to her personal care attendant.

"Okay, Ms. Hattie, I'll go sit in the living room while you rest." Shelia would care for her dying elderly patient half of the day, then Helen would come over most other nights. Secret also pitched in. One thing about it, Hattie knew that she was loved. Her sisters tried to spend the night, but they would just end up fighting. Hattie threw them out on several occasions. As if she were a teenager, Hattie looked around to make sure Shelia was dozing off to sleep in the other room. Then she texted Royce once more to come pick her up. "Just come as close to the window as you can. I'll handle the rest." Royce was so uncomfortable with Hattie's plan, but what could he do? "Son, just help an old lady fulfill her dreams," she previously said.

Royce tapped on the window as if he was a sixteen-year-old boy helping his girlfriend sneak out of her parents' house. Royce frowned as Hattie motioned for him to raise up the window from the outside. She was too weak to raise up the window herself. Giving it a nudge, the window quietly came open. Looking back at the door, Hattie whispered, "Come on, son, be quick about it. Help me get my leg out the window!"

"I can't believe I'm doing this. Your family is going to murder me after they find out what we've done," he whispered while lifting her up in his arms. Royce asked Hattie to place her arms around his neck. She smiled and gave him a gentle kiss on the cheek. "Ms. Hattie, that kiss was sweet, but your family is still going to kill me," he said, smirking.

"Child, I'm already on hospice. What can they do?" Holding out one hand, the old lady said, "Son, give me the keys." Royce shook his head from side to side. "I just want to drive a few miles. It's been a few years, but I can still do it. Come on, hand them over," she said, grinning.

As if they were two teenagers sneaking out to elope, Royce held on to his seatbelt as Hattie screeched out of the driveway. Shelia awoke due to the noise of a screeching loud truck. Her mouth swung open as she saw Royce and Hattie racing down the road. She grunted just thinking about what Helen was going to say when she arrived. "What in the world is that old lady doing?"

Hattie smiled and gave her frowning future grandson-in-law a fist bump. Rolling his eyes, he said, "Granny, I sure hope you're ready for this. Please don't die on me."

Ricky, the skydiving instructor, greeted the two customers as soon as they got out of the truck. "Hey, Ms. Hattie, this big old guy has told me all about you," said the smiling man while extending his hand. Ricky kissed Hattie's hand, and she returned it with a smile. "Are you sure you want to do this?" he asked.

"Well, son, I'm sure Royce told you that I'm living on borrowed time."

He nodded his head and said, "You don't need to say more. I got you. Let's do this!" Ricky motioned for the plane to drive up and pick up these passengers. Royce just sat quietly as he imagined Hattie's heart stopping during the dive, her head snapping back, and finally Secret snapping his neck after it was all over. He didn't know if he wanted to cry or laugh at the moment that the plane went up. He had skydived in the past and was very adventurous before his parents died years ago. Royce looked over and grinned at Hattie because she was strapped to Ricky's chest as if she were an infant. "We're going up fourteen thousand feet, Bobby," said Ricky to the pilot.

"Come on, son, it's going to be okay. Have some faith." Looking over at Royce's face, Hattie patted his hand. He looked terrified because it had been years since he went up in a plane. Suddenly the side door of the plane came open.

"Oh, man, it's time," said Ricky. Due to his daydreaming, he hadn't noticed that he was being forced to jump out of the plane. He wanted to change his mind and call the whole thing off, but by that time, he was being pushed out the plane by another instructor.

"Ms. Hattie, here we go!" Hattie held her arms that were wrinkled with time. She was tempted to close her eyes although she had on goggles. However, something in her wanted to see what she would soon face. At first, her teeth stayed in as she smiled due to the cool crisp air rushing against her face. The land beneath was so green and beautiful. Everything looked so small at fourteen thousand feet. Hattie knew that in a few months she would be flying into the sky to be with Jesus.

As if she were a butterfly flapping her wings, her arms seemed weightless as she stretched them out. There was no fear of dying, leaving her family, or being in great pain at the end. She was so engrossed in her flying that she didn't hear Ricky say, "Ms. Hattie, are you okay? We're fixing to land."

"Whoops, there they go, son!" Hattie's false teeth flew out of her mouth and slapped against Ricky's goggles. Both giggled due to the funny sight.

The landing was smooth, and it looked funny that Hattie looked as if she were running. A small group of employees ran to meet Ricky and Hattie upon landing. The old lady smiled as they clapped their hands and cheered.

"Oh, stop all that fussing. I loved it," she said, shooing them away. Royce had landed just a few minutes earlier.

"Well, how do you feel?" he asked as he helped her get out of her harness. "Where your teeth at, Ms. Hattie?"

"Son, I feel good, and now I truly know how it feels to fly." Hattie was showing her gums as she hugged Royce.

"Ms. Hattie, you are a mess."

Shelia had called Helen, Secret, and all Hattie's sisters. "We need to call the police!" said Helen while ringing her hands. "Hello, yes, I need to report a missing person . . ." Secret rushed over and grabbed her mother's cell phone. "Secret, what are you doing? I'm calling the police."

Shaking her head, Secret said, "Mom, there is no use in calling. Granny has been calling Royce for a few weeks now. They been having all these secret conversations and stuff."

"Why didn't you tell me?" Helen shook her head and shrugged her shoulders.

"Mom, Granny has something up her sleeve, and I know she convinced Royce to do something. Do you remember when she convinced the mailman to let her drive his mail truck? That man got fired after she wrecked it."

Helen rolled her eyes due to knowing that her mother-in-law could be very persuasive when she wanted something really bad. Mae, Jean, and MaryAnn looked at each other and started laughing. "Girl, your granny has pulled some tricks in her day. You know that's true," said Mae to Secret. Lee frowned and squinted her eyes. Jean just shook her head and rocked back and forth. She began wringing her hands.

Lee said, "She is on hospice and should be lying down. I can't believe that Royce would do something like that. We don't even know him that well."

Obviously offended, Secret rebutted, "Aunt Lee, you know that Granny won't do nothing if she doesn't want to."

"Well, I think he kidnapped her and is holding her for ransom," said MaryAnn.

Mae looked at MaryAnn and said, "One thing that I do know is that don't nobody want to kidnap Hattie."

As they were arguing among themselves, the front door slowly came open. The family hadn't even heard Royce's truck drive up. Hattie intentionally drove very slowly so that she and her young accomplice could sneak in the house.

Royce tried to quietly push the door open so that no noise could be heard. However, once he opened the door, he was met with rolling necks, folded arms, and smacking lips turned to the side. Standing there like a deer in headlights, he gave a boyish grin.

"Hey, open the door, son," said Hattie through the door. He had let the door slip out his hand once he realized that he was caught. Hattie came in without her teeth, and everyone noticed that her hair was sticking straight up. "Ladies, and how are you today?" she asked with a toothless grin. Everyone began talking at one time, and it was obvious that they were not happy.

Secret was the only one who noticed Royce's keys in Hattie's hand. She folded her arms, tapped her foot, and glared at Royce as if she could see right through him. "Um, hum," she grunted. "You, me, kitchen, now," she said, pointing at her fiancé.

"Hattie, where in the world have you been?" asked Mae along with her sisters. Just as Secret's great-aunts were giving Granny Bell a verbal spanking, Secret folded her arms and focused her attention on her wide-eyed fiancé

"Royce, where were you and Granny?" Royce looked around the kitchen just to make sure there were no sharp knives around. "You better start talking and I mean now!"

Both of them were cornered by angry women. Royce didn't know what to say. All he could do was shrug his shoulders like a teenager. "Well, what had happened was . . ." Although in two different rooms, Hattie and Royce were pleading their case to their prosecutors. It seemed as if everyone except the two people on trial shook their heads.

"Don't even come with that, Royce Storm." Secret was terribly upset.

Granny Bell yelled at Secret from the living room, "Leave my baby alone."

Secret looked and dropped her jaw. "Excuse me, Granny, I thought I was your baby!" she yelled back. "You just met this man." Turning to the cornered man, Secret said, "And don't think I didn't see your keys in her hand. You let her drive, didn't you?" she whispered."

Now the only man in the room became offended with his future wife. Holding both arms out, Royce said, "Oh, now I'm just this man."

"Baby, you know what I mean, and don't try to turn this back on me," Secret huffed. "Where were you and my granny? Answer that."

Royce blamed the entire event on Hattie, but Secret rolled her eyes as he was talking. In frustration, she marched out the kitchen before he could finish explaining. The two fighting lovebirds returned back to the living room separately. Royce looked like a maimed animal. Hattie finally had to shush them all with her arms as if she was the strongest disciplinarian. "All right, ladies . . . I said, all right, ladies. Okay, I asked my grandson to take me somewhere, and I knew y'all would never shut up about it. Besides, I am close to ninety years old, and I can do whatever I want."

Mae said, "Hattie, where are your teeth? You're on hospice. You cannot do whatever you want. You have a family, and we love you." Mae was visibly upset with her eldest sister and placed both of her hands on her hips. "Hattie, enough of your speech. Where did you go?"

Hattie rolled her watering eyes. "Y'all old ladies make me sick. Okay, I'll tell you the truth." Hattie Bell realized that she was not going to outtalk her sisters. With a deep breath, she quickly said, "Royce took me skydiving."

Royce looked away as he felt several pairs of glaring eyes and dropped jaws. There was no explanation he could give to calm these old fires, nor could he calm the young raging fire that sat beside him. "Now wait, before y'all jump all over him," said Hattie, holding up one finger. "I begged him to take me so I could do some things on my final wish list. He didn't want to, but I begged. Y'all know I don't beg anyone for anything." Royce was so glad Hattie stood up for him because he knew he couldn't beat that rap. Hattie told them that she had an exciting time with her grandson. She continued, "He took great care of me, and I even have video on it. I'm even on the YouTube and the Instant gram."

Helen couldn't help but laugh. "Mom, I know you didn't just say you was on YouTube."

Hattie pulled out her cell phone and showed them that she already had twenty thousand views. "Uh-oh, there my teeth go! Did you see them? They just flew right out and hit the man's goggles." Everyone burst out laughing. "Royce also set me up a Facebook page. Look how many friends I have on here!"

All the anger turned into laughter as they watched the video of the old lady smiling, then toothless, and then flying through the air. "Lord have mercy, girl, you are an old mess." Jean laughed as she saw that her sister was strapped in front of some man's chest.

MaryAnn said, "Hattie, that man is fine! I may go skydiving myself."

"Girl, shut your mouth," Hattie said. "I'm getting hungry. Come on, son. Come on, let's get in this kitchen and fix some food to eat."

Royce looked surprised as Hattie pointed at him. "Granny, I—" he started to say.

MaryAnn interrupted while walking over to Royce, "Man, you know your fine self can cook. Get on in there."

Royce asked Hattie what they were cooking. "Oh, just a little something." Secret laughed knowing that Hattie never did a little something.

"Oh, a little something, huh?" questioned Royce with one eyebrow raised.

"Yes," said Hattie Bell. "I'm thinking about some hot water corn bread, black-eyed peas, some buttermilk fried chicken, candied yams, buttered corn on the cob, and some collard greens."

Royce held his head down and grinned, knowing Hattie took no prisoners in the kitchen. "Well, Granny, I think that's gonna work out just fine."

"Show me what you got, son."

Royce smelled a challenge. "You not ready for this new school, Granny." he jested.

"Aww, shucks, you still got milk on your breath, baby. And I'll show you how we do it down home in Arkansas," Hattie said. All the sisters laughed due to witnessing their sister so happy. No one could touch Hattie's cooking all these years.

With a twinkle in her eye, Hattie took a deep breath. Her head turned slightly to the side as she said, "Girls, now I know what it's going to feel like to fly. I've always wondered what heaven would be like, and now I know. In a few months, I'll have the cool breeze on my face as I taste the wind." Mae, Jean, Lee, and MaryAnn gathered around their eldest sister and gave her plenty of hugs.

"Mom, that was beautiful," said Helen, but Secret quickly walked out of the room.

"Oh, quit your fussing. There will be plenty of time for that. Jean, will you go get my spare set of teeth off my dresser? This old lady has several more things to do."

With that said, Hattie asked Royce to pull her up off the couch so they could fix lunch. Jean said, "Hattie, that ain't no lunch. That's a pre-Thanksgiving dinner."

Secret got herself together and walked to the kitchen. "Granny Bell, what other things are on your wish list?" Hattie pulled a small piece of wrinkled-up paper out of her bra. At first glance, the list appeared simple. Secret wrinkled her forehead, chewed on her ink pen, and then glanced at her grandmother. She shook her head after reading each item.

Hattie basically yelled out her list as Secret was reading through it. "First, I wanted to go skydiving," she said.

Secret huffed and marked that off the list. "Check mark on that one."

"Second, I want you to help me buy red shiny stilettos."

"Oh, now come on, Granny!"

"Third, run a marathon, and don't say I can't!" Before Secret could let out another word, Hattie raised her pointer finger and said, "Fourth, I want to ride in the front seat of a fire truck and sound the alarm." Everyone smiled at that one. Jean knew that was a longtime wish of Hattie's. "Finally, I'm going back home so that I can take my rest, in Arkansas."

Lee, Mae, MaryAnn, and Jean all said, "Oh no, Hattie! Not back to that place." None of the sisters wanted to go back, especially Jean.

"Hattie, there is too much pain there, isn't it?" asked Mae.

"Girls, there is something I want you to see. Will you please talk about it and let me know?" asked Hattie. Jean said she didn't need to think about it. She couldn't go back home, even for her dying sister.

Turning to Secret, she asked, "Baby, can you help me finish my list? I know you have a wedding to plan also."

Shaking her head, Secret said, "Absolutely, let's do it!" With that said, Secret played with Baby Justice while she waited for lunch to be served.

Chapter 7

That Cool March Rain

Royce drove to Dallas every two weeks to see his beautiful fiancée. Royce told Secret how much he missed seeing her at every visit. "I just like seeing you, holding you, and hearing your laugh. Man, we need to move this wedding up!"

Secret hated to say goodbye to her love, but he had to return to Tyler to pick up his daughter, Mercy. They loved each other so much that each visit seemed more difficult to say goodbye. Royce found his future family very appealing. Each member had a story of their own. He had no family of his own, yet he felt comforted that he would be a part of a crazy yet decent family.

The two lovebirds gripped hands tightly as they walked him out to his new truck. "All right, Future Mrs. Storm, I'll see you later," said Royce.

"Do you have to go? I mean you could stay a little while longer," asked Secret as she kissed him softly on the lips.

"Stop kissing me, woman. I have to go. We'll talk more about the wedding later."

Secret rolled her eyes. "You always think somebody is trying to kiss your big old lips?"

He smiled and asked, "Well, aren't you?"

"Heck yeah!" Secret said while kissing him again. Royce had a successful restaurant, a beautiful home, and a daughter that he loved. Life had finally fallen into place. He promised to come back as soon as he could.

Being a restaurant owner made him stay away from home often. There was always some emergency job, but Royce had finally found the Play Safe Daycare Center to take care of his daughter. It was rare, but the staff really sympathized with Royce and his toddler. They had become like family and treated Mercy like one of their own children.

He screeched off out of the driveway, while trying to show off his new midnight-blue Ford F-250. Secret waved and walked to the end of the driveway. She slowly walked backward until she could no longer see his truck.

"Come on back in here, girl! It's pouring down!" yelled her mother from the window.

Secret hadn't even noticed that it had started drizzling. Out of nowhere, the light cool drizzle turned into a cold heavy rain. "I'm coming in."

Royce smiled because he could still feel Secret's lips on his. His mind drifted for just a minute thinking of his future bride and all the love he would have. "Oh, shoot, I'd better put on my seat belt." Turning his head slightly, his arm tugged on the seat belt stuck behind his headrest. The other driver completely ignored the stop sign and didn't even pause. Both drivers seemed to look up at the same time. Royce closed his eyes and gasped as he realized that he could not avoid ramming the truck. He saw the car coming toward him, and all he could do was brace himself. Things seemed to be moving in slow motion as he smelled the rubber from his tires. He felt his face violently striking the windshield. He moaned as he felt sharp pain in his legs. With a whimper, Royce whispered the three most important names that meant more than anything to him. "Jesus . . . Mercy . . . Secret." With one last gasp and one last moan, his entire world went completely and utterly dark.

Secret had lingered out in the rain for a few minutes after her love left her. "Girl, you are going to catch a cold out there!" yelled Helen, opening the door. "I can wash your hair for free if you need your hair washed."

Secret swatted at her mom, but before she could respond, an unsettling feeling hit her stomach. What was wrong? Turning around, she saw flashing lights and heard EMS sirens. The trucks raced down the road with a fire truck following.

Secret's heart began beating faster and faster as she sensed that something was terribly wrong. "Mom, I have to go!"

Helen seemed confused, "Go where? It is raining cats and dogs out here."

Secret stuttered but couldn't explain the very unsettling feeling in her heart. "I don't have time to explain. I just gotta go." Helen grimaced due to knowing that feeling all too well. "Something is wrong with Royce. I just feel it," said Secret tearfully.

"Here's your coat," said Helen as she grabbed Secret's coat off the back of the door. Secret's hands began to shake uncontrollably as she jumped into her SUV and raced about a mile down the wet road. A police officer had arrived first on the scene and pulled a tall muscular man out of the truck. He lay on the wet grass while the officer waited on help to arrive. Secret's mouth dropped as she could see a midnight-blue Ford F-250. "Royce!" she screamed. "Oh lord, no."

No one was touching the man as they were trying to keep onlookers from blocking the road. Running to the battered body, Secret saw the love of her life lying there with no life in him. The officer turned to the onlookers and asked, "Is there a nurse here? Is there a medical professional? The ambulance and fire truck were stuck behind a line of vehicles, and we're having trouble getting through."

Already looking at his body, Secret quietly said, "I'm a nurse."

"What did you say, ma'am?"

As if she was snapping out of a dream, she shouted, "I am a nurse!" Like a robot, she went on autopilot. Suddenly she didn't see her fiancé; she saw a patient. Without saying another word, she bent down and began CPR on the love of her life.

"Count, breathe, pump," she whispered while pushing on Royce's chest. "Come on, babe. You can do this!" Royce was still unresponsive although Secret did all that she could. Her arms were getting tired, and her body shook due to the freezing rain, but she wouldn't stop. Royce lay there unconscious, bloodied, bruised, and lifeless. Secret tried her best to keep it together. She could not imagine losing another man that she deeply loved. What was she going to do?

All she could picture was all her hopes and dreams being ripped out of her hands, again. "No, death again. Please not death again," she wailed. Feelings of desperation and rage came over Secret, and she began slapping Royce in the face. "Wake up, babe, wake up!"

The officer came running over. "Ma'am, ma'am, what is going on here? Do you know this man? I thought you were a nurse.

"Ma'am, ma'am, please step back," said the officer as Secret continued to slap Royce between breaths. Onlookers admitted that it was a confusing scene. The officer bent down and moved the panicked nurse away from Royce.

Sliding backward on her hands, the nurse looked more confused than the onlookers. Secret had gone into a cold, rainy daze. The officer snapped Secret out of her own thoughts. "Ma'am, we've got a heartbeat! But he's still in a lot of trouble." Within moments the EMS had arrived, they transported Royce to the Dallas County Hospital.

Secret followed the ambulance to the hospital. She was now in the seat of the very families that she served on a daily basis. Now, she was being escorted to the trauma waiting room.

"Secret, are you okay?" asked the nursing staff. She hadn't even realized that she had Royce's blood on her hands, shirt, and wet pants. Secret was bloody, cold, and shaking. Another nurse friend of hers grabbed a warm blanket and put it around her shoulders. With wet dripping hair, Secret tearfully said, "That's my fiancé. This is his blood. I'm fine." Gazing into space, she said four times, "I'm fine!" The last "I'm fine" came out as a squall.

"No, ma'am, you're not fine. There's nobody to impress here," said her nurse friend. Before Secret knew it, her friend grabbed her and held her as if she were falling apart. But she was indeed falling apart, and there was no denying it. Secret cried, shook, paced, and kept saying she was fine. Then she would repeat the cycle all over again. Although she did not work at that hospital, Secret had other nurse friends that knew who she was. They could all see that she was not fine.

"We are going to make sure he gets the best care, okay?" said her friend Rosa.

Secret called her mother to let her know what was going on. It had been hours, but finally the ER doctor came out and told Secret that Royce had been placed in ICU. He had suffered a severe traumatic brain injury, possible spinal cord injury, and a few broken ribs. "More internal injuries are yet to be determined," said the doctor. Secret's ears heard what the doctor said, but her brain could not comprehend the depth of his injuries. By the time she reached the ICU room, all she could do was collapse in a chair. Her love had tubes, IVs, and bandages on every part of his body. She grabbed his hand. Although it was warm, it was like a lifeless heavy weight.

"We had to place him in a coma to give his brain time to heal."

After talking to a family attorney, Mr. Matthew Smith, Picket was on cloud nine. She really didn't need a family attorney, but hired him just in case she ran into trouble. Since there was no custody agreement, then both of Mercy's parents had equal rights to her. All she had to do was go pick up her child if Royce would give her up.

"I know it sounds simple, Ms. Jones, but these situations can get ugly," said Attorney Smith.

"Well, Mr. Smith, Royce has never been interested in our daughter. The only time he showed interest was when he had met some woman last year. She seems to care for my daughter, but I am her mother."

Mr. Smith asked Picket if she knew where Mercy was, but she didn't know. "Well, I hope all turns out well, but call me if you have any problems."

Not only did Picket have a desire to go get her daughter, she also had plenty of money to fight with. After all was said, Picket gassed up her car and headed to Royce's last known address.

Secret was pulled out of her thoughts due to her cell phone ringing. "Ms. Bell, this is Sabrina from Play Safe Daycare. You are listed as the backup contact if Mr. Storm could not be reached." Nodding her head, a gentle tear fell from her eyes. "We have been calling him for hours but can't seem to reach him. Mercy has been here over the allotted time. Is anyone coming to pick her up?"

In all the confusion, Secret had absolutely forgotten that her future stepdaughter was still at daycare in Tyler, Texas. "Oh lord! I completely forgot about Mercy. I am so sorry." Secret explained the situation to the daycare attendant. "Please just keep her there until I can get there. I am on my way." Although it was practically a two-hour drive, Sabrina informed the daycare staff of the situation. Everyone stayed there with the toddler.

Picket grew frustrated while driving around her own hometown, in Jefferson. She had been in jail for what seemed an eternity, and every street looked new to her. She shook her head while driving by her old drug hangouts. "Oh no, I didn't know the bed-and-breakfast had closed," she whispered while driving. The building was now some kind of restaurant. "Hmm, Royce, what did you do?" Getting out of her car, Picket looked around her former community, and it had all changed.

"Excuse me, sir, did this use to be a bed-and-breakfast?"

"Oh yes, Mr. Storm was the former owner of both." The young man told her how Mr. Storm had turned his bed-and-breakfast into a restaurant. He was kind of a celebrity around Jefferson. "Can I help you with something?" he asked.

She gave a faint grin, admiring how much the place had changed since she was there last. "Yes, I'm looking for Mr. Storm. Do you know where he is? I need to get a message to him," she said while picking up a cookbook with his picture on it.

"Well, since he sold the place, we have a new owner, but I think Mr. Storm moved his new restaurant to Tyler."

The last time Picket had seen Royce was when he was grossly overweight, leaning on a crutch, and huffing for air. In this picture, Royce was tall, dark, muscular, and handsome. "Is this Mr. Storm?"

"Yes, that's Mr. Storm. That picture gets the same reaction from all the ladies," said the young man, smiling.

Picket nodded her head in agreement and disbelief. "Shoot, if I would have known he was going to be that fine, I would have kept him for myself," she whispered.

"Did you say something, ma'am?"

She shrugged her shoulders. The guy at the front desk looked through his cards and handed it to Picket. *I guess I'm driving to Tyler today,* thought Picket.

Picket had been driving a little over an hour before she reached Tyler. Part of her felt stupid because she didn't even know where to start looking for Royce in this East Texas city. "Oh shoot, I need to get some gas," said Picket as her gas light blinked on. Stopping at the gas station, her mouth swung open as she walked slowly by a *Tyler Daily Newspaper.* There was a large picture of Royce on the front page alongside a mangled truck.

"Ma'am, you have to pay for that," said the cashier. Picket hadn't even realized that she had grabbed a newspaper and headed toward the door. The headlines read, "Restaurant owner hanging on to life."

"Oh, I'm sorry. Give me thirty dollars on pump 6 and the newspaper," Picket said to the cashier while her eyes were still reading the paper. Shaking her head, she read how Royce had been in a near-fatal car accident in Dallas. *I guess I'm driving to Dallas then.* She was already determined to pick up her daughter, but now she really needed to find her daughter. Picket's hands shook as she turned the keys to the ignition. She didn't know if Mercy was in the car with her father or who was taking care of her. "Just take a minute and breathe," she said to herself. Picket decided to use the coping skills she had learned in prison counseling. She opened her bottle of cold soda and ate a few Doritos.

"Excuse me, lady, could you please pull up a little bit?" asked a lady while tapping on Picket's window.

"Are you talking to me?" asked Picket with offense.

"Didn't I tap on your window? Just because you have a shiny Navigator doesn't mean you can park in two spots. Are you getting gas, or are you eating? I said pull up!"

Both rolled their eyes at each other as the lady walked into the gas station to pay for her gas. The lady looked familiar to Picket, but she didn't have the time to focus on it.

In frustration, Secret pushed the gas station door open. "Geez, folks are so rude these days." Secret gasped as she grabbed the newspaper from the rack. "Royce, babe," she said while wiping a tear. The *Tyler Daily Newspaper* had a picture of Royce on the front cover. She still was somewhat in shock. "I need twenty-five dollars on pump 5." Secret had to get some gas on her way to pick up Mercy from daycare. "There's a rude lady hogging up the gas tanks. I just thought you should know," said Secret to the cashier. After paying for the newspaper, she walked quickly out the door.

Picket was still pumping her gas as Secret walked back over to her car. Secret looked at the lady pumping gas on pump 6. She looked familiar to her, but she didn't have time to focus on it either. "Thank you for moving up your car," Secret said as she motioned with slow hand movements toward the flustered lady.

"Lady, I don't have time for your foolishness today. If I wasn't saved, I'd take these hands and . . . ," said Picket as she got into the car.

Rolling her neck, Secret yelled, "Well, I am a Christian, and you better be glad that I know him!"

"You don't know nobody," Picket mumbled.

The women both cranked up their vehicles and drove in two different directions.

Chapter 8

Double Take

Secret arrived at the daycare around eight in the late evening. In a near panic, she said, "Oh my goodness, I'm so sorry. I made it as quick as I could." She had parked in front of the door and left the car running. "Hello, is anyone in there?" she shouted, banging on the glass door. The daycare was dark and closed, but she continued to bang on the door. Secret heard a buzzer that unlocked the door. In a hurry, she ran into the building, swung the door, and looked into several classrooms.

"Shhhhh, come on in," whispered a daycare worker. Secret huffed while trying to catch her breath. She calmly tiptoed over to her sleeping future stepdaughter. "Hello, Ms. Bell, my name is Gina. I'm the one that you spoke with on the phone." Although Gina held out her hand for a shake, Secret hugged her. "We have all prayed for Royce as soon as we heard the news. It's been in all the papers today," said Gina.

"He's in really bad shape right now, but I am praying for him." Although she tried to keep a strong front, a flood of gushing tears fell from Secret's eyes as she bent down to pick up Mercy.

Gina had packed her little Hello Kitty backpack with plenty of pull-ups, sippy cups, snacks, and clothes for Mercy. Placing her hand on Secret's shoulder, she said, "I know you will take loving care of her. Royce has told us all about your love story. You mean so much to him and Mercy. He also told us about the time you saved this baby's life from her mother."

Unpleasant memories surfaced into Secret's mind. "Girl, I bet not ever see her face around here, again. Anyway, we are going to be a family. Only God could have done this." Gina asked Secret if she minded her praying for her. "You don't even have to ask me that. I don't ever turn down prayer. You know we could definitely use it now."

"Father, in Jesus's name, I ask you to watch over this family and heal Mr. Royce. I pray that you give Secret all the strength she needs to turn this pain into power. Keep them safe, amen."

"Thanks so much for the prayer."

Mercy continued to sleep during the ride to Dallas. She didn't know anything of the day's events. She had no knowledge that her father had called her name before his world went dark. She raised up and saw her future stepmother driving. Mercy didn't know where they were going, but she didn't care. It had indeed been a long, horrible day. Secret was so exhausted by the time she made it home. She struggled to carry Mercy and all her bags into the house. "Girl, you are getting so heavy."

The toddler had stayed with her future stepmother multiple times over the last few months. No matter where Mercy was in the house, she would find her way to Secret's bed. The next morning, Secret would wake up to Mercy and Baby Justice with their legs on her back. Sometimes the future siblings would be cuddled together, and other times someone's little foot would be in Secret's side. Oftentimes, Secret would wind up on her own floor. "Okay, that's it. Both of you are getting your own toddler beds," said the tired mother. Although she didn't live there permanently, Mercy had her own Peppa Pig toddler bed. It was placed right beside Justice's Superman toddler bed. Admittedly, the room had become crowded, but that was fine.

The night passed without much commotion, but Mercy did wake up and get in the bed with Secret. Secret started to wake up the kids early, but she decided to sneak out of the room and have a cup of coffee. Decaf was her usual, but she drank fully caffeinated vanilla flavored on this morning.

"Good morning, baby," said Helen upon seeing her daughter.

"Morning, Mom, before you ask me how everything is going, let me take a few sips of coffee," said Secret sleepily. Helen had fixed breakfast for her daughter before she went to work. "It's bad, Mom. Really bad. I don't know what to do. If I think about it too long, I'm going to have a meltdown."

Helen placed her arms around her daughter's neck. "This is not the first time you have gone through a hard time, darling."

Secret nodded in agreement and said, "I know, but I sure was hoping it would be the last." It was so much going on checking on Royce, taking care of Mercy, working, and helping her grandmother fulfill her bucket list.

Secret decided to take a week off work and called her cousin Monica to come over and watch the kids. She called the Dallas County Hospital to check on Royce. There was no change this morning. Royce would be in a coma for a few more weeks. Hopefully his brain would reduce in swelling, and he would regain consciousness. "I'll be up there later," Secret said.

Then she called Granny Bell and Shelia. Granny asked how her grandson-in-law was doing. There had been no change and no point in wasting the day away. Secret told her she was going to check on him later that evening. "All right, Granny, put your clothes on so we can go to the mall. Can Shelia get your wheelchair out?"

Frowning, Granny said, "Uh, I don't need no wheelchair yet. I can still walk on my walker."

"Granny, that is too much walking for you to do. Tell Shelia to get the wheelchair. I'm on my way," said Secret.

"Shelia, my bossy granddaughter is on her way to take me shoe shopping. Please get my wheelchair ready." The wheelchair had to be cleaned up because it had not been used in years. However, Hattie hated to admit it, but her health had declined in a few short weeks. She was getting winded very easily, and it was getting harder for her to stand.

"Okay, Ms. Hattie. I'll get your chariot ready for takeoff."

Secret, Hattie, and Shelia had an enjoyable day at the mall. "Okay, Granny, let's find some shoes for you." Hattie pointed to the Jimmy Choo shoe store and indicated that she wanted to go in. "No, ma'am!" Secret already knew that the shoes in that store were very expensive. Secret tried to take Hattie to other cheaper stores, but Hattie refused.

"Secret, I said Jimmy Choo."

"Granny, what do you know about Jimmy Choo?" asked Secret to a determined Hattie.

Shelia laughed because she had been helping Hattie look on different websites for shoes. "This had been in Ms. Hattie's mind for a while," said Shelia with a grin. She tapped Secret on the shoulder and said, "This is what she wants."

"Granny, you are a mess." Although Hattie was in a wheelchair, she tried on at least ten pairs of high heels. Finally her eyes lit up as she saw a red pair of glittery stilettos with a big lace ribbon on the back. Secret wiped her eyes then shook her head after looking at the price under the shoe! "Granny, these shoes are nine hundred and seventy-five dollars!"

Hattie just nodded her head and kept right on smiling. "Get my purse, Shelia, these are the pair I want." Secret was startled that her grandmother still wanted the shoes. Hattie gave a smug grin. "What are your wedding colors?" Hattie asked her shocked granddaughter.

"You know, Granny, I hadn't even thought about that. Royce and I had not even discussed wedding colors with everything going on."

"Well, would you consider wearing red shoes?"

Secret just rolled her eyes. "Red! Really, of all the colors . . . ," huffed Secret.

"Well, Secret, we already know you're not gonna be wearing white. For heaven sakes, this is your second wedding, and you have a child," said Hattie.

"Granny, we all know this. Thank you so much for that." Hattie asked the attendant to bring out six pairs of shoes. Secret didn't know whether to faint or to hold her chest. "Granny, are you serious?"

"Secret, pick out any pair you want."

Secret could hardly speak as she asked, "Where did you get the money?"

Hattie frowned. "Just pick out some shoes. Don't be asking me all those questions. Now go on and model for your granny."

As if she were a runway model, Secret strutted down the shoe aisle. "These are the ones, Granny!" It was the same pair that her grandmother picked out.

"See, I knew you had good taste. Now we're twins." Secret rolled her eyes when she remembered how Hattie used to dress her in matching clothes. Neighborhood kids would laugh at Secret because she dressed like her grandmother.

"All right, woman, let's go." With that said, both ladies left, smiling with brand-new shoes. "Granny, I don't know if I want to give you a 'you go, girl,' a high five, or spank your bottom." Secret asked Hattie what she was going to do with shoes that she couldn't even walk in.

"As much as these shoes cost, I'm going to wear them night and day," said Hattie. She wanted to wear them every day.

"Lord have mercy," said Secret. "Granny, I wish I could get inside your head. Where did you get that amount of money to spend on shoes?"

Granny Bell didn't answer, but Shelia told Secret that her granny was not broke. Pulling out the list, Secret said, "All right, that's two down, Granny. Next, I will see how in the world you are going to run a marathon in a wheelchair.

"Oh, baby, I'm not going to be using my wheelchair."

Secret rolled her eyes and took a deep breath. "I'm not even going to discuss this with you now, woman. I've got to get to the hospital," said Secret.

―――――――

"How are the kids?" Secret asked Monica. Justice and Mercy had both been playing and eating good all day. Of course they both loved watching the toddler channel. "I've just pulled up to the hospital." Secret stopped by the nurses' station to speak to the hardworking nurses.

"Oh yes, Mr. Royce's sister has been in there all morning. She is so nice," said Nurse Carla.

"Uh, Royce doesn't have a sister," responded Secret with raised eyebrows.

Carla said, "The young lady said she was family, and she has been holding his hand and wiping his face all morning."

Secret briskly walked to the room while Carla was still speaking. Looking, she saw no one in the room except her sleeping fiancé. Maybe the young lady had left. A flush was heard coming from the restroom. She quietly took a seat on the other side of Royce's bed. As if a chilly wind came into the room, both women's jaws dropped as they came face-to-face in Royce's hospital room. "Didn't I see you at the gas station in Tyler? What are you doing here?" Secret asked the woman. The woman asked Secret the same thing.

Flabbergasted, Secret said, "Royce is my fiancé, and I already know he has no sister." Both looked familiar to the other one, but at first, they could not exactly place each other. In a flash, Picket remembered the pregnant lady that fought with her at the park last year. Each took a long hard second look at each other.

"It's you!" they both said, pointing at each other. Although each lady had given their lives to Christ, each needed deliverance from fierce tempers.

"How dare you bring yourself up in here after what you did! I ought to slap the taste out of your mouth . . . Jesus help me right now."

Picket was not backing down. "This isn't what you want."

Secret stated while rolling her neck, "Well, since you said you're going to come over here and slap somebody, then get to slapping." It was obvious that both women knew there was going to be a fight when Secret quickly took out her diamond-studded earrings. Quickly pulling back her long shiny hair into a ponytail, she walked upon Picket.

"Royce must have given you those nice earrings because he gave me the same pair a few years ago." Picket smirked while swinging at Secret. Secret fell over Royce's legs trying to claw at Picket. One open-handed smack reached Picket's face. Picket's fist reached Secret's right eye. One of them stepped on Royce's blood pressure monitor sensor. Carla rushed in to cut off the alarm, but she did not know that she was in the middle of a fight.

"Good lord, ladies, please stop fighting in here! Y'all are laying on Mr. Storm!" Carla yelled while pushing Picket out of the way. She could hardly believe her eyes. Both ladies seemed to forget that they were in a hospital room. As if it were a brawling street fight, the ladies were punching, pulling, hitting, and rolling all over the room. Secret's perfectly manicured long hair was being pulled by Picket. Picket's beautiful light-brown skin was being bruised by Secret's closed fists. Carla acted as if she were scolding two young children. Picket stopped fighting when she realized that she accidentally smacked Royce upside the head. Carla yelled, "My gosh, the man is already in a coma!" When

Secret saw that her fiancé had been smacked, she became more enraged. "All right, that is enough. Security! Security! Get out of here!" shouted Carla out of the room door. The intense tussling continued while security was on the way. The nurse just stood there with both hands on her hips, tapping her feet.

"I still owe you some licks from last year," roared Picket to Secret.

"I can't believe you remember anything since you were high on crack and all!" Picket's jaw dropped since that statement was a painful reminder of her past. She punched Secret even harder. Just then, Officer Jackson came limping down the hallway as fast as he could. He was seventy-three years old with two bad knees. One of his diabetic shoes started to slide off the back.

Carla said, "Now you know we needed a little more help. No offense."

"Well, I was just filling in today. I actually retired last year," said Officer Jackson. "I'll do what I can in there.

"All right, ladies, break it up. This is not the time nor the place." Like an Oreo cookie, he tried to pull them apart. However, he was no match for the two fierce lionesses. They continued to struggle, but this time Secret fell over Royce's chest. She fell on the bed monitor, and his feet went up in the air!

"Oh, baby I'm so sorry," she cried.

"Look at you, trying to kill my man already." said Picket.

"I know you just didn't call Royce your man?" asked Secret as she pulled Picket's long ponytail. Just then, a six-foot-eight, three-hundred pound security guard came rushing in.

"Thank god, we needed you at first," Carla barked. "Move these two into the family room, please," demanded the flabbergasted nurse.

"Let my hair go and I'll let your hair go!" Secret huffed. With that said, both ladies were escorted forcefully to a private room while still pulling each other's long ponytails.

Neither woman could fit through the door because they were holding the other one's hair. "Okay, kindergartners, on the count of three, you both let go," said a voice from inside the room. Each cautiously released the other's hair. "Sit down, you two!"

As if they were in the principal's office, the ladies gave a quick glance toward each other and then glanced away. Both ladies sat back in their seats with their arms folded.

"Who wants to be the first to start?" Michelle was Royce's nurse case manager and a licensed social worker. "Do both of you realize that you each struck a man in a coma? Maybe they should have called an exorcist instead of a case manager. We need to cast the devil out of the room." She said this looking at both of them. "Now look, I can see that both of you obviously care for Mr. Storm, but y'all know better." There was a complete hush across the room!

Both ladies were somewhat embarrassed after the adrenaline wore off. "I cannot believe that you showed your face around here again," said Secret while leaning into Picket's face. She then put her finger into Picket's forehead. Obviously, Picket was offended and swatted her finger away from her face.

Secret's fierce anger had calmed down; it came back raging at this moment. Secret said, "You better be glad that I am a Christian, lady. But I am going to break that pretty bony finger of yours."

With a smirk, Picket said, "You sure don't fight like a Christian."

Michelle gave each lady a cold bottle of water. "Maybe this will cool the two of you hot tempered ladies off."

After taking a long sip, Secret said, "I am a Christian, but you done got me messed up.

"Uh, you threatened to slap me first," said Picket.

Michelle said, "Well, I am glad we are all women of faith here, but ya'll are a mess. If I was Jesus,

I'd hold my head down and keep on walking past both of y'all. Both of you seem to care for Mr. Royce. But if I didn't know any better, I'd think you were trying to kill the man and finish him off." Both ladies held their head down in obvious embarrassment.

Michelle turned her attention toward Picket and said, "You told the staff that you were family, but I found out you are not related to Mr. Storm. So can you tell me why are you really here?"

Secret looked at the lady being questioned with her head turned to the side. "Oh yes, Ms. Picket, tell us why you are really here."

Michelle glanced at Secret all side-eyed because she was over this foolishness. "Excuse me, Ms. Secret, are you an attorney? Well, then let me ask the questions please, if you don't mind." She shrugged her shoulders like a child and then took another sip of water. Picket explained that she was in town to pick up her daughter, Mercy.

Spitting out her water, Secret shouted, "I know you didn't come here to pick up nobody!" She began rocking back and forth while holding on the chair arms. Both of her fists clenched at the same time, and she clenched her teeth! "Lord Jesus, if you do not help me right now! You mean the same baby that you tried to sell for drugs. Do you mean the same baby that you kicked under a car? Do you mea—"

"All right, Secret, we get it" said Michelle, trying to make sure the women stayed apart.

Picket held her head down and took a deep breath. "I am ashamed to say that I did all those bad things. I do not know if Mercy will ever forgive me, but I deserve another try. I was on drugs really bad, and I lost hope, but now I've turned my life around."

Secret stood up and gave a sarcastic handclap. "Oh, that's so great. Oh, you have turned your life around. Great, awesome, wonderful, but you are still not taking Mercy!"

Picket became increasingly agitated. "Look, I know you're Royce's so-called fiancée and all, but you will never be that little girl's mother."

"Oh, you mean the little girl that calls me Mommy," said Secret while rolling her neck.

This time Picket began to pray out loud. "Lord, you see this woman. You see I'm about to kill someone in this very hospital! Help me, Father, because I do not want to go back to jail."

Michelle listened as Picket shared all she had been through in the last few years. Secret then explained all that she had been through last year. It was obvious that both of them had experienced a lot of trauma in their own lives. Both women needed grace and understanding for each other. Now, a little girl was in the middle of all this.

Picket looked at Secret with understanding. "I really am sorry for the loss of your husband, but obviously you've found a replacement!" said Picket. Secret rolled her eyes. "You are not the only one who has lost a child, though. I know personally that it can be rough."

"Thanks for that, I think," said Secret.

Picket cleared her throat. "Besides, any woman that can fight in three-inch red Jimmy Choo stilettos has got to be a tough girl." Secret had forgotten to take off her wedding shoes. She felt kind of embarrassed not realizing that they had been on the entire time. "With that being said, you are still not keeping my daughter. Where is she anyway?"

Secret frowned and said, "I'm not going to tell you anything. Royce put my name down as an emergency contact."

"An emergency contact is not the same as a parent. Oh, so you have her at your house, don't you?" Picket asked with her head to the side.

Just then, Michelle received a call on her work cell. Royce was crashing in the other room. The ladies stopped arguing, and all ran to Royce's hospital room.

Chapter 9

It's Your Move

"Ladies, you have to stay out here," said Michelle. Usually she wouldn't have gone in during situations like this, but with everything going on, she ran inside. Royce had gotten a blood clot, and it was heading to his lungs. He was in bad shape due to having a massive heart attack as a result. The doctors were barely able to get him back from the grave. He needed surgery immediately.

"Ladies, I really hope you can stop bickering long enough to pray for Royce," said Michelle as she slowly came out of the room and closed the door behind her. "We almost lost him." Michelle looked at her pager that beeped. "He is in critical condition. Technically he could go either way. Hopefully with prayers and good doctors, I hope he will be fine."

Picket looked at Michelle and asked how long she thought Royce would be in the hospital. "Well, I really don't know. I'm not the doctor, but his condition is life threatening," she said while walking backward down the hallway. "I've really got to go. I need y'all to work this out for the man hanging on to life, and his little girl could be fatherless if things worsen." As if Michelle were a scolding mother, she pointed at both of them. "No more bickering, fighting, or name-calling between you two." As if both of the ladies were teenage girls, they rolled their eyes as the lecture continued. "This is a serious situation, and both of you claim to be women of faith. Use your faith and pray for this man."

Although there was no love lost between them, they both shook their head with understanding. Picket looked at Secret. "Where's Mercy?" asked Picket in a calm yet confrontational tone. "That's my daughter, and I'm taking her back to Jefferson with me." "Oh no, ma'am, not today, you're not taking her anywhere," responded Secret. Picket ruffled through her purse, obviously looking for something. Secret backed up and asked, "What are you gonna do? Shoot me?"

Picket grumbled, "Girl, ain't nobody thinking about shooting you, but if you would have caught me before Jesus, I would do just that."

"Then what are you looking for?"

Picket found her attorney's card and handed it to Secret. "I don't have time to fight anymore with you today. I am tired, and you have literally worn me out. Here's the card for my attorney." Secret looked at the front and back of the business card. "But tomorrow you'd better have my daughter ready to go."

Secret placed one hand on her hip and smacked her lips. "Well, Miss Thing, you're not the only one with an attorney, if you just want to do that," she said.

Granny Bell called Secret at the very moment that she thought about pulling the rest of Picket's hair out. "Baby, what is going on? I can hear the tenseness in your voice."

Walking down the hallway, Secret left Picket standing in the hallway. Picket walked back into Royce's hospital room and took a seat. Secret continued talking on the phone to her grandmother while getting inside her vehicle. "I can't even begin to tell you how angry I am right now!" she shouted inside the car while banging both hands on the steering wheel. "Granny, can you believe Mercy's mother was up here at the hospital with Royce and—"

Hattie said, "Catch your breath, honey."

Secret continued to tell Granny Bell about the terrible events of the day. "We were fighting up in the hospital and even hit the man that we both obviously love. It was terrible, Granny," said Secret.

"Secret Lakeshia, I thought you were saved."

With a smirk on her face, Secret said, "Granny, I'm still working on it. I haven't been that mad in a long time." Hattie told her that she would have done the same thing in the situation. "They don't know us, Granny. We don't play, do we?" They both laughed and agreed to see each other later that evening.

Although she tried to focus on other things, the future bride cried all the way home. She wanted to focus on her wedding, her grandmother's hopes, and her fiancé. However, images of sweet little Mercy kept flooding her face. She didn't have her own attorney, but Secret did have important friends in her arsenal against Picket.

"Octavia, hi, this is Secret. Are you still a supervisor at Child Protective Services?" Octavia Harris told her that she had been promoted to the program director since she saw her last year. "You better go, girl," said Secret. Octavia Harris had become acquainted with Secret and Royce last year after Mercy was returned to Royce. The entire town knew the story of how Secret basically saved the child's life. "Well, you told me to call you if I ever needed help with Mercy. So I am calling," said Secret to Octavia. Secret gave her a complete rundown of the day's events and how Picket had come back to get her daughter. Secret said, "I need to ask you a serious question."

"Okay, anything."

Not only was Octavia a program director at the department, she was very good friends with the local district attorney and all the family attorneys. If anyone had inside information of how these situations worked out, surely Octavia knew.

"Royce is in a coma, and his recovery date is unknown. He is so unstable right now that I don't even know if he is going to make it," cried Secret on the phone.

"You can't think like that, Secret, because he is going to come out of it. Tell me, who is taking care of Mercy now?" asked Octavia.

"Me." Octavia continued to listen as Secret made her case. "How can Picket just come back in her life and demand that I give her up? I mean she doesn't even have custody of her daughter. Royce does!" The more Secret talked about it, the more upset she became.

"Okay, now just calm down," said the quiet lady on the other end.

"And then she demanded that I meet her somewhere and drop off a child that doesn't even know her. How in the world is this legal? Can't Child Services do anything? Y'all were the ones who took Mercy from Royce." Octavia began chewing on a wad of gum. She could hear the stress and anxiety in her friend's voice. "Octavia, are you chewing gum while I'm talking?" asked Secret skeptically. "Please say no, because you told me that you only did that when you had a tough case."

Octavia took a long pause then asked, "Has it been proven that Picket is an unfit mother since she's gotten out of jail?" Secret didn't know why that should matter. Octavia continued, "Yes, we placed Mercy back with her father after he did everything he needed to do." Clearing her throat, Octavia said, "But Picket's parental rights were never terminated, and she probably had a great attorney. I shouldn't even be talking to you about this."

Secret became silent and then started sucking on a peppermint that she found in her purse. With a long sigh, Secret said, "I don't even know how long she's been out of jail. I don't know where she's living because she just showed up out of nowhere." Secret asked Octavia if she needed to get an attorney to fight this battle. It was difficult to say, but she did not need to get an attorney just yet.

Octavia asked Secret to hold while she made a few calls to the courthouse. "Okay, sorry for the long hold. I called about two of my family attorneys that I know. They both looked in the system for any custody papers, court orders, or something that would help you. Just like I thought, she had a heck of an attorney on this one. It appeared as if Picket had done everything she needed to do to get her daughter back. While in jail, she got clean and took parenting classes, counseling, and other things to get her daughter back. Somehow the charges of child endangerment were dropped, and only the drug charges stuck."

Secret began to shout over the phone, "She can't just pick up her child after all she did to hurt her!" It was a harsh reality, but since Royce and Picket were never married and there was no custody agreement, that's exactly what was going to happen. Both parents had done all they needed to do to get Mercy back.

"Child Services is no longer involved with this family. Secret, I hate to tell you, but the child's mother has every right to come and get her child, especially since the father is incapacitated right now. I've checked, and there's nothing in place to say that Picket cannot come pick up her child."

"What does that mean?" Secret asked a question that she already had the answer to.

"I mean you have to let her go with her mother. I am so sorry," said Octavia. "However, if you can prove that Mercy is being abused or neglected by her mother, then call us, but you'd better not be making no false report." Tears ran freely down Secret's cheeks. What could she do? "I'm going to be very honest with you, Secret. If you don't turn Mercy over, Picket has every right to come with local police and have you arrested for kidnapping." Flabbergasted, Secret yelled, "That's ridiculous! I'm going to prove that Picket is unfit! I'm going to investigate myself!" Then she hung up the phone.

Secret was furious, but she knew that her friend was telling her the truth. It was just too hard to imagine Mercy being taken by a woman who tried to sell her for drugs.

The beautiful big-eyed baby girl that was literally abandoned and dumped at her father's bed-and-breakfast over a year ago. Mercy even called Secret her mother, and she loved her so much. Royce was near death, and now the closest thing to her love was being ripped from her arms.

———

Picket was rambling through Royce's papers inside his hospital drawer. "Hmm, thank God for this," she said. Secret's phone number had been written down as the next of kin.

Picket sat by Royce's bed, squeezing his hand. "Royce, can you hear me?" she asked to the sleeping man. "I'm so sorry for the words that I spoke to you. I was really messed up the last time that we saw each other." Shaking her head, Picket visualized their last meeting at the park. She was high on drugs and was in the process of selling her child. "Love, I've asked God to forgive me, but I've never asked you. Please forgive me for all the pain that I have caused you and our baby girl."

Picket gave a slight grin thinking of what her two-year-old must look like now. Wiping a tear, she whispered, "I want you to know that I forgive you too. I forgive you for not being there for me when I really needed you. I forgive you for leaving me alone."

The nurse walked in as Picket was confessing her love for Royce. She hoped that they would be a family again. *Lord have mercy, the drama in this room, right here,* thought the nurse as she went about her duties.

"I've got to go. I am going to get our daughter back. All of this is my fault," she cried. "Okay, I'll see you tomorrow. Do you hear me?"

Clearing her throat, the nurse said, "Madam, I'm sorry, but since you are not family or on the next-of-kin list, you can't come back. So sorry, Ms. Secret said you are not on the visitor list."

Picket huffed and snatched her purse and walked out. "Oh, we'll see about that."

Literally exhausted from the events of the day, Secret returned home in the late evening. She walked past everything and collapsed into her bed face-first. "Mother, I'm home," she whispered. This bride had taken her grandmother shopping, she had checked on the love of her life, and she had a physical altercation with her fiancé's baby mother.

Helen knocked on the door. "Honey, are you forgetting something?" As if he were a sleeping bag of potatoes, Helen gently lay Baby Justice in his mother's arms.

Secret flooded him with endless kisses. "Oh, Baby Mama, love that baby's apple cheeks."

"I have one more thing for you," said Helen.

Helen brought in a sleeping toddler with big brown eyes and fat thighs. Although well into her second year of life, Mercy still gave slobber kisses. "Girl, I was sure you'd been asleep by now." Mercy opened her mouth wide and gave her future stepmother lots of kisses. Helen told Secret that Mercy had been awaiting for her to arrive. She refused to go to sleep even for a minute. "Come on, Big Momma, it's me and you tonight."

Her eyes became blurry with tears as Secret said, "I love you, sweetie. I'll never let you go."

A wrinkle appeared in Helen's forehead, wondering what was going on.

"Mom, something terrible happened today." Secret gave Helen a play-by-play of the events of the day. "And, if I don't give her up, I could risk being arrested for kidnapping!" she squealed while blowing her nose.

"Oh no," said Helen. "Well, we can't solve this tonight, but if she comes over here with that foolishness, we got something for her."

Secret wiped her nose. "Mom, we have to let God handle this. I tried to handle it today and wound up hitting my man in the head. I almost got thrown out of the hospital." Helen and Secret both giggled thinking of the fight.

"I shouldn't be proud, but I am. Girl, you took it to her in those high heels." Helen smiled and shook her head.

"Mom, cut it out. I can see God has a lot of work to finish on both of us," said Secret while patting her mother on the shoulder.

"You've got that right." Helen turned off the lights and gently closed the door. Mercy snuggled closely into Secret's side as Baby Justice lay comfortably on his mother's chest. Usually Secret would gently rise up and place both children in their own toddler beds, but tonight was different. Instead, she held them as close as she could. Mercy's huge cheeks were kissed over and over because Secret knew that was probably their last night together.

Chapter 10

In God We Trust

Secret's phone rang loudly. Sunlight shone through the blinds in her bedroom. The alarm went off at the same time that her cell phone was ringing. Still somewhat disheveled, Secret picked up the phone with her eyes closed. "Who is calling me this early? Hello, whomever you are, it is Saturday," she barked with frustration. Both of the children were still sleeping soundly.

"Hello, Secret, have you had a chance to talk to your attorney yet?" asked Picket smugly.

Secret hated to admit, but she was going to have to meet with Picket. "Yes, I've gotten legal counsel, and that's all you need to know," snapped Secret.

"Well," said Picket.

"Well what?"

Picket huffed and said, "Lady, you are really trying my patience. I'm sure if you had proper legal counsel, then you already know that I have every right to have my daughter." Although she knew it was true, Secret didn't want to admit that she had to give Mercy back to her mother. This was indeed an ice-cold conversation.

"So what do you want to do?" asked Secret to Picket.

Picket told Secret to meet her at the Dallas County Hospital parking lot. They agreed to meet at ten. Picket knew Mercy's future stepmother was not going to stand in her way. She had to take one last verbal jab at the lady on the other end. "And she better be clean too," she said.

Secret was almost completely outdone. "You know what, I am not even going to respond to that comment." Being a fairly new Christian had multiple good points, but she prayed that God would excuse her while she told Picket a thing or two. "You don't know me or your daughter. I have taken care of her since she was eight months old. I could say a lot more, but Jesus won't let me."

Picket told Secret that she had one more thing to say before they got off the phone.

"What is it?" said Secret with a tired sigh.

"I think you should know that Mercy will never be your daughter."

"Well, that's a lie because I am marrying her father."

"No, ma'am, you are not because I'm not just coming for my daughter, I'm coming for Royce too. We are going to be a family again."

Secret dropped the phone due to pure shock. "I know you didn't just say what I think you said. You're coming after who?" All Picket could hear was rumbling on the other end of the line and Secret praying very loudly, "Lord Jesus, I need you right now! This woman done lost her mind." Mercy and Justice both woke up due to Secret's loud ramblings. Picking up the phone, Secret yelled, "Sista, you almost made me lose my religion."

Two-year-old Mercy Storm had no idea what was going to happen that day. She was so happy to be at her second home with her future little brother. Secret held her very tightly and smothered her with kisses. "Baby, this is gonna be a day." Obviously Mercy did not understand what Secret was talking about. She grinned, hugged her, and gave the tearful lady plenty of slobbery kisses.

Helen walked slowly into the room. "I heard all the commotion, and, baby, I am sorry." Helen could see that her daughter was about to blow. She hadn't had an outburst like that in a long time. Handing her a tissue, Helen said, "As if you haven't been through enough already . . . Let it out now so that you won't make a scene when you get there." With that said, Secret allowed the fear, rage, panic, and anxiety to all come out at once. She cried over losing Mercy, but also the possibility of losing Royce. The children began to cry loudly. Secret didn't mean to scare either one of them, but she had to get out her tears now.

"Why Mommy cry? Why Mommy cry?" asked Justice in his one-year-old dialect. Of course, his mother understood his questions. Before she could answer, Mercy climbed up behind her neck and said, "Mommy, get better. You hurt?" Then she gave her wet kisses on her neck.

"Mercy, pray for me, girl . . . I need it," said Secret. Mercy looked at Secret as if she didn't understand, but without warning, she slapped Secret across the forehead. "Jedus . . . Jedus . . . name." Justice started jumping up with both his little arms raised like they did in church. Although she wanted to keep crying, Secret couldn't help but to laugh hysterically. "You guys are a mess." Helen laughed as she witnessed both children trying to comfort Secret. "So this is what it boils down to. My prayer partners are two toddlers." It was a poor attempt to comfort their mother, but that's the best they could do.

Helen said, "As weird as it seems, I think God actually understood the prayers of the children." They all gave each other a big family hug before putting on the kids' clothes.

Secret looked at her watch as she waited in the parking lot with Mercy. "I don't even remember what she is driving," mumbled Secret as she looked out her car window. The toddler just kicked her feet in the back and quietly played with her toys. Although she wasn't talking, Secret cried quietly.

"What wrong, Mommy? Why cry?" asked Mercy.

Secret ignored her question and wiped her eyes. She looked into her lighted mirror to ensure that she left no tearstains on her cheeks. Surely, Picket would never know that Secret cried over losing Mercy. One wouldn't think that this loss could compare to her losing her unborn baby three years ago or losing her husband last year. However, this entire situation was completely different. There was a certain bitterness to giving up a child that she considered her own. Secret's mind drifted even as she checked her makeup in the mirror. *I mean it's not as if we're exchanging phone numbers or recipes. I can't believe that I am sitting her fixing to exchange a child.*

A black Lincoln Navigator pulled in the parking lot across from Secret. She hated to admit that Picket's shiny detailed Navigator was a lot nicer than her dirty red Ford Explorer. In all the business of life, Secret hadn't had time to clean out her car or wash it, for that matter.

"All right, little lady, it's time for you to go with your mother. Never mind the fact that she . . . well, you don't need to relive all of that." Secret was tempted to go into much more detail than she needed. Besides, she could tell Mercy had no idea what she was talking about. By the time Secret turned back around, Picket was standing there tapping on her window. "Girl, you scared me."

Picket gave a sarcastic grin. "You better be glad I didn't key this old Ford. Besides, you don't look like the type that scares easily."

Vulnerability was not Secret's strong point, but Picket could see that she was struggling to open her door. "Couldn't we at least warm up to this?" Secret asked.

"No, don't drag this out. We have to go home." Picket could see her now toddler through the car window. "She's gotten so big and so beautiful. Look at my baby." Picket cried with her hands cuffed over her mouth.

Secret hated to unlock her door, but she did. "You might as well take her out of her car seat."

Mercy looked at the lady who was so unfamiliar to her. She didn't even recognize who was taking her out of her car seat. Was this a new daycare worker? Was this one of her father's friends? Not having the vocabulary to ask questions had its downfall. "Hi!" said Mercy with excitement.

"Well, hello there, sweetie," said Picket while kissing her daughter.

Secret didn't know whether to throw up or just turn away. Something in her made her witness the entire scene, although she wanted to run away. Everyone was out of their car. Secret leaned backward on her driver's side car door.

"She likes me," said Picket to Secret.

"She still doesn't know you."

Picket attempted to carry Mercy to her vehicle, but the toddler jumped down and ran back to Secret. "Mommy!" squealed Mercy. Secret stood there with her head hung down. Picket walked briskly over to Mercy and grabbed her up in her arms. "Mommy, come!"

"Baby, I can't come."

Picket ignored the fact that Mercy called Secret Mommy. "Hey, baby, I'm Mommy. I'm your mommy. Come on now, we have to go."

She may have been two years old, but this toddler realized that she was being taken by someone she didn't know. Why was this happening? Who was this woman taking her from the only mommy that she knew?

"This is ridiculous!" Secret screamed out. "Can we work anything else out?"

Although Picket was now wrestling to lock the kicking toddler in her seat, she yelled out, "No! Now leave us alone!"

Secret couldn't stand there and watch her soon-to-be daughter kicking, clawing, fighting, and crying. Mercy was inconsolable. Heartbroken, she continued to reach out both arms to Secret. "I can't watch this," cried Secret. She jumped in her Explorer and screeched out of the parking lot.

The weeping lady only made it a few miles down the road before she had to pull her vehicle over. Her eyes were so blurry that she had pulled over to wipe her face. "Lord, I don't know how you gonna work this out. But I want to trust you. I trust you even when I don't know what you're doing." Her prayer was not pretty. It was not eloquent; it was full of yelling to high heaven. "God, you've got to help me! The man I love may die, and my daughter was just basically kidnapped," she sobbed. As if a warm blanket came over her shoulder, Secret could feel divine strength coming from on high. She sensed that no matter what was going on in her life, God was with her.

Pulling over to a gas station, Secret decided to call her mother.

"Mom, it was so awful!"

"Girl, it sounds like it. I can't even imagine how hard that was on you. So what are you going to do now?"

"I don't know, but if she thinks she's seen the last of me, she has another thing coming," Secret said.

"There you go. That's my baby. In the meantime, the bridal shop called because you missed your fitting this morning."

Secret gasped and said, "Shoot, with all this going on, I forgot all about the fitting. Mom, do you think I should put everything on hold?"

"No, just keep planning. You need to take it one day at a time. I suggest that you go and get yourself a good hot cup of coffee."

With a tired sigh, Secret said, "You know what, Mom, that's the best idea I've heard all day.

"I hope that planning the wedding and helping your granny will help you refocus. By the way, your granny already called this morning."

Secret rolled her eyes at her mother like she did when she was a teenager. "I don't feel like talking to anybody right now."

"Well, you'd better not let your grandmother hear you say that. You're not too old to be put across her knee.

"I'll tell you what. I'll take Justice to the children's zoo today. He's going to get a real kick out of the baby animals." Helen laughed due to thinking that her grandson was a real cutup. "So don't even worry about him today."

Helen told Secret that she needed to take an official leave of absence from her job. But Secret wanted to work a little longer so that she could keep herself busy.

Secret felt like taking a long drive just to clear her mind. She turned up the radio, grabbed a vanilla latte from Starbucks, and then put her shades on. Looking straightforward, she decided to drive to Tyler. *I need to check the mail at the restaurant. I'm sure there are important messages by now.* Secret drove but also daydreamed, cried, and sang with the radio down the highway. The Secret Place Restaurant looked decent on the outside. Someone had put a note on the door that the business was closed temporarily. It had been a little over a week since Royce had his accident. *I haven't called the employees or anybody*, she thought while unlocking the door.

Secret and her fiancé had talked about a lot of things concerning their future, but they had yet to discuss the restaurant. Of course, the restaurant was named after her, but she technically wasn't his business partner. Was she? *Oh lord, there's so much to do. Well, at least they cleaned the place before closing out.* Secret had been there many times and knew where all the business information was. Slapping her hand on her forehead, she decided to go through all the bills. One particular bill got her attention. It was from the Galaxy Bank dated over a month ago:

> Mr. Storm, we thank you for your business. However, you are now five months behind on your rent. We will be forced to foreclose on your loan in thirty days if you fail to make your payments.

Secret leaned back in Royce's chair. "Babe, why didn't you tell me!" she said in frustration. He owed more than seventeen thousand dollars to the bank and several thousand dollars to his employees. It was obvious that Royce had been sinking financially for months. "There's no way we are going to save this place!" Royce had not told Secret that he hadn't sold many books lately and his savings had run out. He was headed for financial ruin.

She decided to call the employees and assure them that they would get paid as soon as possible. Secret felt relieved due to everyone being understanding for the time being. Everyone was understanding except the bank, but she would deal with that later.

I can't think about this now, so she locked up and sped off. Secret had fixed up Royce's home since she was thinking about moving into it. The struggle continued as to whether she was moving to Tyler with Royce or staying in Dallas to pursue her career. She smiled as she opened the rose-colored mailbox that she and Mercy had painted. It was full of bills and letters from those who liked Royce and those who did not. "Oh, this is nice," said Secret, opening the first letter. It was a letter from his pen pal, Davis Patton of the US Marines. The letter stated that Davis was being discharged soon. He'd be there in time for the wedding, in August. *I still hope there's a wedding by the time you get here,* thought the mail woman. He was excited to finally meet Secret, the lady that Royce was going to marry. "Thanks for finally sending me a picture of your girl. She is stunning, man." Secret didn't know if she should be impressed by the compliment or horrified that Royce sent her picture to another man. He was also asking Royce for more information about his adoption. He was feeling really lonely and wanted to know how Royce was coping with no close family.

Chapter 11

Believe I'll Run On

The day had completely flown by before Secret realized that she hadn't even called to check on Royce that day. She hoped that her love would come out of his sleep. The wedding was in five months, and barely anything had been done. They didn't even have a place to have the wedding. There were no flowers, no caterer, and no groom. The only thing she had was a beautiful white wedding dress. *What if there is no groom? What if he dies? What if...* There were so many racing thoughts in her mind. These days her focus was scattered between losing her grandmother and possibly losing her fiancé. Secret wanted to trust that things were going to be well, but to be honest, she really didn't know. Pulling out her cell phone, she decided to look at her Bible app. As if God were talking to her himself, in the Explorer, the perfect scripture appeared at the top of the page. She read it out loud so that her ears could be comforted. Psalm 46:1 read, "God is our refuge and strength, a very present help in trouble." A warm feeling of peace rushed over Secret, and instead of anxiety, she only felt stillness.

"Hello, who's the charge nurse this evening?" asked Secret, calling the hospital.

"This is Dorisha. I'm the charge nurse this evening."

"Oh, pleased to meet you. I know it's by phone, but I hope to see you later." Over the next twenty minutes, Dorisha went through Royce's chart. They discussed his blood work, lab results, recent tests, and all things medical. Being a PA herself, Secret knew everything to ask for. However, Dorisha reminded her that she was not on duty.

"We got this, Ms. Bell. Don't worry, we will take good care of Mr. Storm. If there are any new changes, I will call you," Dorisha said. He remained asleep, and the swelling in his brain hadn't gone down. "Yes, Ms. Bell. I know, Ms. Bell. Hmm." Secret seemed to ask her every question under the sun. "Yes, he is getting physical therapy. Ms. Bell, Ms. Bell, his treatment team is handling things," responded the charge nurse with frustration. "Ms. Bell, I have to go now. I will call you if there are any changes, okay?" Dorisha finally received an "okay" from Secret.

Hattie Bell had been on hospice for a few months, and although there weren't many physical changes, her health was slightly declining. Her legs seemed to grow weaker by the day, and now she traveled more in her wheelchair than her walker. She was aware that the Dallas City Marathon was coming up in a week, and she hoped that her granddaughter was able to secure her a spot in the marathon. On her drive back home, Secret asked God to give her a plan to help fulfill Hattie's dream. *Lord, I don't know how we are going to pull this one off, but I know you always have a plan.*

"Shelia, how is Granny today?"

"She is doing as well as can be expected. This week she is spending most days in bed or in her wheelchair." Shelia whispered on the phone, "Secret, how in the world are we going to help this woman run a marathon? I know this is going to be a miracle, if we can pull this off." Shelia cleared her throat and looked around the room for listeners. "Secret, you know they had to put your granny on oxygen. She keeps taking the nasal cannula out of her nose. You know she fought tooth and nail, but don't tell her I said anything," she whispered on the phone.

"Girl, I don't know how that woman is going to run a marathon especially with an oxygen tank. Me and my big mouth."

Both of them shook their heads on each end of the phone. "Let me talk to Granny." Shelia handed the phone to Hattie due to hearing her loudly talking and coughing in the background. "Hattie Bell, you stop all that fussing before I get my switch," said Secret playfully to her grandmother.

"Oh, baby, Granny just feeling bad today."

"I know, but guess what?"

"What?"

"We are on track for the marathon in a week," said Secret cheerfully. "Lord, please forgive me for lying," whispered Secret under her breath. As if someone opened up a bottle of cheer, Hattie let out a loud coughing laugh. "By the way, did you know that a full marathon is twenty-six miles?"

"Yes, and I'm still going to walk across the finish line."

Secret rolled her eyes due to knowing that there was no way Hattie would be able to run twenty-six miles.

"Girl, I have faith in you."

"Granny, are you sure we can't just roll you across the finish line in your wheelchair? I can see someone running while pushing you in your chair."

"No, I want to walk across the line. Now, baby, I know you are going to figure it out."

"Granny, how are you going to run a marathon?"

"Lakeshia, you are lovely." Smiling, Secret told Hattie that she hadn't called her by her middle name in years. "Hold on, baby, the home health nurse is here."

Secret started to hang up but decided to eavesdrop on the line. She had a long drive anyway, so she may as well listen.

"Ms. Hattie, how are you today? I already heard that you were not wearing your oxygen like you're supposed to. Are you taking all your medicine?"

Hattie huffed, buttoned her lip, and turned her head toward the closet. "Rosa, you already know that there's no point in me taking medicine. Y'all just trying to make me comfortable. Well, I'm not!"

Secret giggled hearing her grandmother. "Show out like that."

Hattie coughed every few minutes but continued to fuss. "So why are we prolonging it! Y'all, let me go." Secret could hear someone turning on Hattie's oxygen. "Get that thing off me!"

"Shelia, could you come in here please. Maybe you can talk some sense into Ms. Hattie," said Rosa while opening Hattie's room door. Shelia came into the room and reminded Hattie that she had a wedding to attend and a bucket list to complete.

"Granny, Granny, stop all that fussing! Keep that oxygen on! You want to breathe, don't you?" yelled Secret in the background.

"Oh, baby, I forgot you was on the phone."

"It don't make no sense, you acting like that. If that were me, you'd spank my hind end, wouldn't you?" Secret reminded her grandmother that she couldn't run a marathon if she didn't take all her medicine or have her oxygen.

Like a scolded child, Hattie said, "All right." Secret felt her mood lighten, and she smiled and sang all the way home.

The next morning started with a desperate prayer and a hot cup of coffee. "Dear Lord, thanks for this lovely spring day. You know that the Dallas Marathon is in less than a week, and I have no ideas." Secret took another sip and cleared her throat thinking of the lie that she told Hattie. "I know you heard that tale I told Granny, but your girl was desperate. Please give me a plan." After praying, she put her head down on the table. "Father, I'm grasping at straws here." Just then her cell phone rang. *Who in the world is calling me now? I don't even want to talk.*

"Hello," *said Secret.*

"Hey, girl, this is Evon. I know we haven't spoken in a while, but you came across my mind." Evon told her that she heard about Royce's accident and just wanted to check on her.

"Thanks so much. Girl, my stress is out of this world. We need to get together for lunch and catch up sometime."

"I would love to see you soon, but I am so busy at the Make-a-Wish Foundation. We have request coming in left and right. It's sad really, but that's why I help."

"Did you just say that you help at the Make-a-Wish Foundation?"

"Yes, I think I found my purpose! I know that God has called me to help families. My job is to link terminally ill children with any resource to make their dreams come true."

"God is good. I think you are an answer to my prayer. I know y'all work with children, but do you think you could help a terminally ill elderly person?" Secret told Evon all the recent events concerning her grandmother and what huge gift she had been to the community.

"You know what, I think we can help. I will talk to my supervisor, okay?"

"Thank you, Lord!" Secret yelled over the phone. Evon laughed and told her to calm down. She would call her in a few hours with a definite decision. Time passed quickly, and before she knew it, Evon called her with good news. The Make-a-Wish Foundation would contact the Dallas Marathon Association. They would "bend all kinds of rules" to make Hattie's dream come true.

"Okay, Secret, I've already come up with a plan that you are going to love." Evon told her that over fifty volunteers wanted to run for Hattie. "I know it's not a relay race, but the Dallas Marathon Association will allow it, in this case." She would figure the distance that each person would run until the last few feet. "Please talk to your family about it. I really think your aunts could play a significant role in getting their sister across the finish line."

Secret pointed one hand to the ceiling and said, "Thank you, Lord. You did your thing." Although she had done a lot of crying lately, this time it was out of pure joy.

"One more thing," said Evon. "Since it is a five-hour marathon, I suggest that someone bring Hattie only for the last thirty minutes of it."

"That's a great idea. I would have never thought of that."

Not realizing that she had been in her robe all day, Secret hurried off the phone due to the doorbell ringing. "Mom, can you get the door?" asked Secret as she put her clothes on in the restroom. It was her aunts Mae, Jean, MaryAnn, and Lee. "Oh, ladies, I'm so glad you are here. I was going to call y'all anyway. I've got great news on the marathon." She filled them in on the plan to help Hattie Bell cross the finish line.

"We can do it," they all said at the same time.

"Can you imagine a bunch of old ladies crossing the line?" asked May to MaryAnn.

"Y'all are the old ladies. I still got some fire left in this here tank."

Lee smiled and said, "Come on, girls, let's go buy some orthopedic Skechers at the mall?"

It was an extremely exciting week for the entire family and the volunteers. Hattie had no idea of anything going on, and she didn't know that so many people had heard her story.

"Wake up, sleepyhead. Today is the big day," said Shelia to Hattie.

"I've changed my mind. I don't feel like running today. I am hurting so bad."

"No, ma'am, you can do this, Ms. Hattie. Besides, if you start taking your pain medicine like you're supposed to, you wouldn't be getting in that level of pain."

"Oh, shut up, Shelia. I'm not doing it," said Hattie, rolling back over then pulling the covers over her head.

"Ms. Hattie, you don't have to finish the list that you wrote. Although you're the one who wrote it, we understand if you want to throw in the towel." Hattie's home health aide walked into the other room while leaving Hattie's bedroom door open. With a somewhat smug grin on her face, Shelia plugged her cell phone to the house speaker. Helen had connected the house speaker to play in Hattie's room. Knowing what she was doing, Shelia put on an upbeat old-school gospel song called "I Believe I'll Run On."

Granny rolled back over and glared at Shelia with a grin on her face. "Oh, you had to go put on the Mighty Clouds of Joy. That's my favorite song."

"Really, I didn't know that, Ms. Hattie. Ain't that something?"

Of course Shelia did know that. "All right, lady, you win. Grab me a few pain patches off the dresser, would you? If I'm going to run today, I need some breakfast and a pain pill," said Hattie while swatting Shelia.

"That's the spirit, Ms. Hattie."

Shelia dressed Hattie in black shorts and a bright neon shirt, and of course, Hattie demanded that she wear her sparkly red stilettos.

"Lord have mercy! Ms. Hattie, you can't cross the finish line with those shoes on."

"As much as I paid for these shoes, I'm wearing them every day and every night."

All of the volunteer runners wore the name Hattie on the back of their shirts. By the time Shelia pushed Hattie close to the finish line, the race was nearly over. Everyone was already in place, and Evon told the entire family that Hattie had arrived.

"What's going on here?" asked Hattie to Secret.

"Well, Granny, you said you wanted to run a marathon, and everyone here is running in your place. All you have to do is cross the finish line."

A huge grin came across Hattie's face as well as tears streaming down her eyes. Hattie grabbed her granddaughter's hand and kissed her engagement ring. "You know what, baby? When I gave you this list, I didn't know if you were gonna be able to help me."

"Oh, Granny, come on now."

"Baby, I'm gonna cross the finish line!" Hattie could not hold back her emotions. She started bouncing in the wheelchair and waving her arms. "Hallelujah!" yelled Hattie as she burst into song. "When I've crossed the finish line. I'm not saying that I did all I could. I'm just saying that I did the best that I could. I'm ready to cross the finish line." Her voice trembled with every word, but she sang loud and strong. Hattie was actually thinking about her earthly race in this life. She just wanted to hear God say, "Well done!"

"You better sang your song, sis," said Lee, walking closer. With that said, Hattie looked up and saw a crowd of people walking in her direction.

Seeing MaryAnn, Jean, Lee, and Mae in their orthopedic running shoes made Hattie burst out in laughter.

"What in the world!" she hollered.

Her sisters walked up and surrounded her wheelchair. "It's time to cross, Hattie," said Mae, reaching out her hand.

"Now, Mae, you're almost as old as I am. How am I going to lean on you?"

"We are all going to help you finish your marathon."

With Secret on Hattie's left side and Helen on her right side, they lifted her out of the wheelchair. Shelia grabbed Hattie's walker and placed it right in front of her patient.

"Oh, I don't want to use my walker. I'm going to walk on my own. Even if it's my last day of walking."

Knowing that Hattie was no longer able to hold up her body, Shelia whispered something in Secret's ear.

"Go, Hattie, go!" yelled the crowd. Hattie waved as if she were a superstar and gave a thumbs-up. Like a rocket ready to take off, Hattie tried to raise up her legs, but she couldn't. "Ms. Hattie, we are going to stand you in the middle of the line." Hattie cheered as each of her sisters, Shelia, Helen, then Rosa took a few steps each. Each one had passed the baton to each other until they reached Hattie. "It's time," said Rosa.

"Girl, where did you come from?" asked Hattie to her home health nurse.

"Ms. Hattie, now you know I had to be here, just in case you passed out or something."

"Hush your mouth." Hattie laughed. With all five of their arms locked, and with Rosa and Shelia putting their hands around her waist, Hattie and her sisters crossed the finish line taking one small step at a time. Although this was not a movie, today's ending couldn't have ended any better. Secret stood on the sidelines wiping tears from her eyes. Reaching into her pocket, she pulled out her notepad and then crossed off one more thing off the list.

Chapter 12

When Love Awakes

Secret's phone rang about 8:00 p.m. "Hello, Secret, this is Dorisha."

"Did something happen?"

"Oh no, I just have great news. Your fiancé woke up about four hours ago."

"What?" Secret squealed!

"Yes, I was checking his blood pressure, and when I turned around, I saw two big old hazel eyes looking at me!"

Dorisha told her that they had to run several tests just to make sure that the swelling in his brain had gone down. "So far he's remained awake." Secret breathed a sigh of relief while clutching her neck. Dorisha continued, "The doctor just wanted to make sure that he was okay. That's why I didn't call you at first, but he is alert and looking around." Secret asked if he was saying anything.

"Not yet. Can you come in the morning? The therapist wants to see how he responds to you."

"Uh, yes, I will definitely be there."

The family was excited to hear the news about Royce's awakening. The next morning, she awoke earlier than usual. After Justice was dressed,

Secret fixed herself a large latte with her new coffee machine. "Bye, Mom, I'm on my way to the hospital." Helen kissed her grandson as Secret placed him in the bed beside Helen. Secret almost ran several red lights trying to get to the hospital. The corners of her lips seemed to be smiling on its own. "Hey, everybody," Secret said while briskly walking past the nurses' station. All the nurses smiled due to knowing her good news. "Hey, handsome," she quietly said upon entering his room. "So you finally decided to wake up and see what was going on?"

Royce glanced at her and simply said, "Hey."

Just then, Dorisha came in the room. "This morning, he has said very little, but the fact that he's saying something is a great sign of recovery. Isn't that right, Mr. Storm?" she said while taking his blood pressure.

"Ms. Bell, my name is Dr. Rowland. I am the neurosurgeon whose been keeping an eye on Mr. Storm. I heard that this guy has a wedding to attend in a few months." Dr. Rowland began shining a small light in Royce's eyes. "Although we'll be taking it one day at a time, we are going to work very hard to get him up and running." He asked Royce to follow his finger with his eyes. "Mr. Storm, we still have a long way to go. You've been asleep for a few weeks. How do you feel?"

Royce looked slightly confused and responded, "Fine. What happened to me?"

Dorisha told Secret that she didn't want to wear him out, but he could have visitors for a little while. "In a few days, we will start intensive therapy and then assess him to be moved to another room."

"Lunch is served, Mr. Storm," said the nurse aide, smiling. "You haven't been able to eat since you've gotten here weeks ago." Everyone knew that Royce was a master chef and hoped he would like the food there. The charge nurse had already told her to report how he tolerated lunch.

"You seem to be doing pretty well with that food," Secret said, while she spoon-fed him Jell-O. She continued to talk while she told Royce all the events of the previous day. She told him about the list that Granny Bell had made and how she planned to help her reach her goal. "Can you believe that I'm doing this all while planning our wedding? Honey, do you still want to get married?" she asked, leaning close to his face.

"Yes, you're' pretty," Royce said while rubbing her cheek.

"Roy Storm, you are a hoot."

Secret told Royce that she wanted to cancel the wedding for now but push it back to the following year. "What do you think? Babe, we have a lot going on right now."

"Sure, that's fine. I like you at Christmastime."

"Royce, you are not making any sense, but I am taking it as you agree to cancel the wedding for now. I will tell everybody when the time is right," she said.

Royce smiled and said, "Yes, when the time is right."

For the first time in a long time, Secret had several mixed emotions. She was so happy her love was awake and alert, but she couldn't help but notice the faraway look in his eyes. As a nurse, she knew that this was common for someone with a brain injury. Royce still didn't know what was going on or how he ended up in the hospital. Being a well-trained nurse, Secret was aware that she and Royce had a long way to go and a lot of therapy needed to take place.

Will you be all right? she thought to herself as she kissed his hand. Royce began to fall asleep as Secret tried to give him a detailed account of his accident.

Just then, Dorisha came in. "All right now, I think Mr. Storm needs his rest." Secret agreed and quietly left the hospital.

With her brain full of question marks, she eased into her vehicle. Was she still getting married? *Is this wedding even going to take place? We still don't have a place to get married,* she thought as she wiped her tears. *Come on, lady, get yourself together.* Secret's phone rang just as she started to cry loudly. *My lord, I can't even have a meltdown around here.* Part of her wanted to laugh just imagining herself having a balling squalling fit in her car. It was not the first time it had happened.

"Hello," she said while blowing her nose.

"Hey, baby," said Granny Bell.

"Good afternoon, woman! How are you doing?"

"Well, baby, you know me. I'm doing all right."

"Granny, would you tell me if you were not doing all right?"

"Nope, of course not."

Secret knew that her grandmother always had a reason for calling. "So, baby, I was wondering how are we gonna get me on a fire truck? You got any ideas?" Secret shook her head because she hadn't even thought about it. "Well, baby, we're planning a dinner this evening. Why don't you come on over and we can discuss it then, okay? The girls are already in there cooking."

"Okay, Granny."

Secret came home and told her how Royce was doing.

"I know he has a long way to go, but at least he is doing good for now," said Helen.

"And how is my little big man?" Secret bent down and picked up Justice. She made a rumbling noise as she kissed him on his chubby cheeks. "Mom, what's the dinner about?"

"I think you already know what the dinner is about," said Helen.

Secret held her head down. "Yes, it's getting close to that, isn't it?" She'd been through so much already, and she just couldn't imagine losing another love to some kind of tragedy.

Helen told Secret that Hattie had been talking about her funeral all week, and she wanted the family to know what she wanted. "She also asked me and Shelia to do her a special favor."

"What favor? I'm already doing all the favors."

"This one is special, but I'll tell you more later. Speaking of her final wishes, Secret, do we have a fire truck for her to ride on yet?"

"No, we just got finished with the marathon. I haven't even had time to work on a fire truck."

Helen told Secret that she dated a fireman a few years ago. He was now the fire captain. "Let me make a phone call and see what I can do."

Secret gave a faint grin and shook her finger at her mother. "Now, Mom, don't be doing no special favors around here," she said jokingly.

"Girl, hush. Stay out of grown-folks business. I'm just going to make a simple phone call. If I just happen to ask if the man is still single, then I will let you know."

"All right now, don't make me spank those hips."

"Secret, I'm saved, sanctified, but I'm still looking."

"Well, make that call, Momma, make it," Secret said while placing Justice back in the playpen.

Secret began humming a familiar tune while taking a shower. Her lips turned downward as she recalled that she used to sing that tune with

Mercy and Justice. Two-year-old Mercy had been gone with her mother for a few weeks. Her toddler bed still sat in Secret's room because something in her heart felt that she'd always be back.

"I can't think about that today. I hope she's doing fine." Come to think of it, she hadn't heard anything at all." Secret had not forgotten to go check up on the child, but she had to put that on the back burner. Everyone had to focus on Hattie's last few months. Getting dressed, Secret thought, *I can't imagine losing another person that I love.* She hadn't let herself feel the grief because she had been too busy.

"Shelia, we're here," said Helen upon opening the door. It was already unlocked because Hattie's sisters were already there in the kitchen.

Secret gave Shelia a hug. "Thank you again for moving in with Granny." Helen reached to give Shelia a big hug because they all knew what was going on, and they all knew why they were there.

"Where's the food, y'all?" Secret asked while walking toward the kitchen. Her aunts quickly showed her out and sat her at the table. "Aunt MaryAnn, this table looks fabulous."

Just then, Justice waddled over and raised his little arms toward his great-aunt Jean. "What do you want? Ain't nobody gone pick your big old self up," she said while reaching toward Justice. He took off running, and she chased behind him.

The house was filled with smells of old-fashioned cooking and a large vanilla candle. "What did y'all do in that kitchen?" asked Hattie as Shelia rolled her to the table.

"We just threw on a little something, Hattie," said Lee. "We got some meat loaf, mashed potatoes, with brown onion gravy, green bean casserole, fried cabbage, fresh buttermilk corn bread, some fried chicken wings, and candied yams." Lee smiled while quoting the menu to her sister.

Hattie smiled and said, "I sure raised you girls right."

"Well, Granny, they aren't exactly girls," she said, laughing. Dinner was filled with laughter and sharing old memories. Hattie told Secret things that she didn't know about her aunts. They had a lot of troubled times, but so many good times. Mae told Secret how Hattie would make them dance to "My Girl" by the Temptations when they were sad." Helen laughed as Mae, Lee, and MaryAnn tried to demonstrate by swinging their arms side to side. Jean was noticeably quiet when everyone else spoke about the past. Secret noticed that she just kept eating and looking in her purse.

"Come on, let's go to the living room. I want to talk to y'all," said Hattie. Shelia wheeled her then helped her sit in her favorite recliner.

"Remember what we talked about in the kitchen," whispered Lee to MaryAnn.

Secret overheard Lee and whispered, "What are you two cooking up?" Lee told Secret just to go with it because they had something special for Hattie. They were going to teach her a lesson. "This should be interesting after the last few days I've had," Secret said with a sinister grin.

Hattie leaned forward in her chair and asked Shelia if she could hold her hand. "Girls, this is really going to be emotional for me. My time is getting close, and I want to tell you what kind of homegoing that I want."

Helen said, "Mom, we already know what you want and how you want it. You do realize that you won't actually be there, don't you?"

Mae chimed in, "Sis, I know that you want a small homegoing with only close friends and family."

Hattie held up one finger and ordered them not to do a lot of crying because she would be in a better place. "Ain't no use of y'all carrying on. You know, I don't want all of that. This will be a celebration of my life."

Just then, Lee began to holler out, "Oh, Lord have mercy. My sister is gone. She's at that great kitchen in the sky." Hattie was taken off guard because she didn't know why Lee acted that way. Jean began tearing at her shirt and pretended to faint.

MaryAnn rushed over to fan her. "She just couldn't take it no more. Oh, Lord, Hattie, why did you have to go? You were so young!" squealed MaryAnn.

Hattie told them to stop all that foolishness. "Y'all better not be doing all of that at my funeral." Hattie swatted at Jean and Lee.

Helen began flapping her arms like a chicken and began singing, "I'll fly away!" As if that wasn't enough, Secret fell to the floor and began to crawl on her hands and knees.

Hattie couldn't take it anymore and began to laugh uncontrollably. "Oh no, not my baby. Are you in this too?"

Crawling around on the floor, Secret yelled, "Granny, why? She was just a baby in her prime."

Hattie Bell yelled out, "Excuse me, the old lady was almost ninety, for goodness' sake! Shelia, do you see all this foolishness? All y'all are getting a spanking with my shoe." Helen winked at Shelia and motioned for her to speak.

"Ms. Hattie, you know I would never let that happen. But I would ask Pastor Thompson to give you a rousing send-off. I'll make sure he wears those skinny jeans and muscle shirts that you love so much." Everyone knew that Hattie hated when Pastor Thompson wore those skinny jeans on youth Sunday. She felt that it was highly inappropriate for the pastor to try to "act younger than he was."

"Shelia, you better shut up. I'll be rolling over in that coffin if he preached my funeral in those jeans." What started off as a somewhat somber family dinner turned into an evening filled with joy and laughter.

The lady on hospice couldn't hold on to her frustration because she couldn't stop laughing. Her sisters shook, flailed their arms, ripped at their clothes, and really put on a show for Hattie. Mae calmed everyone down from their laughter. Walking over to Hattie, she said, "Sis, you know we love you, and there is nothing you can tell us that we have not already thought about. I promise that you will have the best homegoing service in the great state of Texas."

Lee interjected, "There will be beautiful flowers and scented candles."

MaryAnn told her that several people would give loving speeches, and only the best singers would be there.

Shelia handed her patient a box of tissue to blow her nose. She was crying at the love she felt from her crazy family. Jean leaned in and kissed Hattie on her cheek and said, "Thank you, sis, for all you did for us."

Hattie wiped her eyes and blubbered, "Y'all have made my day today. Even with all this foolishness." She pointed at her granddaughter and said, "You know better. I better not see you crawling on the floor. I will come back and haunt you." She laughed while shaking her finger at Secret. Shelia connected her cell phone to the house speaker and began to play "My Girl," by the Temptations. Mae, Jean, MaryAnn, and Lee danced their way and surrounded Hattie in her recliner. Hattie was truly their girl, and she bounced in her chair for the rest of the song.

Chapter 13

Visiting Regret

It took Secret and Helen three weeks to arrange a fire truck adventure for Hattie. They would arrange a truck ride when there wouldn't be much action around the city. It would be next week during the Spring Bluebonnet Flower Parade Downtown. "That's perfect timing, Captain!" said Helen with much excitement.

"You know that you don't have to call me that, Brown Skin," said Captain Welding to Helen. It was obvious that these two had some sort of past relationship. Helen's ex-boyfriend Captain Floyd Welding agreed to allow Hattie to have her ride in the fire truck. After talking to his fire crew, they all thought it would be a good idea. After all, some of them remembered Hattie from cooking for the whole station a Thanksgiving dinner a few years ago. Captain Welding had eaten many meals when he was dating Helen a few years back. Although things didn't work out with Helen, he still wanted to do something nice for the "old sweet lady." As a matter of fact, Hattie Bell had been a big part of the community for many years. She had made down home food for policemen, firemen, and doctors; and nearly half the community had been nursed at her side. Everyone heard about her being on hospice, and they all knew that she would be dearly missed.

"What's the plan, pretty lady?" asked Captain Welding to Helen.

"Since the parade starts at noon, I suggest you pull the fire truck up to the house about eleven thirty."

"Okay, Brown Sugar, I'll be there with the crew. Oh, one question."

"What is it?"

"Did you ever get married?"

"No, I'm not, but I am still waiting on the right man to come snatch me up."

"All right now. I'm still single too. So, baby, I'm on my way."

Helen didn't want to admit it, but she was smiling deep inside. She was proud of Floyd and all his achievements. In the past, he had been too busy with his career to settle down and get married. Who knew, maybe they could work something out this time. Anyway, Hattie Bell was the focus today and not an old boyfriend.

***

"Good morning, Ms. Hattie. Have you gotten all your beauty rest out?" asked Shelia while slowly turning back Hattie's covers.

"Hey, baby. I had a rough night. I don't think my oxygen tank is working properly."

"Well, Ms. Hattie, you know that it's not the oxygen. It's your lungs that are getting a little worse." Hattie just held her head down and began rubbing her hands together.

"Are you in any pain, Ms. Hattie?"

"Just a little, but I'm okay."

Shelia began singing, "I woke up this morning with my mind, stayed on Jesus." She bounced over to Hattie and began getting her dressed. "Ms. Hattie, look what Helen bought for your special day today." Shelia pulled out a red, white, and blue jogging suit. It was a little windy.

Hattie smiled and told Shelia that she loved the outfit. It would look so good with her shiny red stilettos. She struggled to breathe, so Shelia adjusted her oxygen levels, but her spirit was still strong. Shelia could see that Hattie was getting weaker, and she knew that she had a few months. She would do her best to make it the most wonderful few months that Hattie had. She had been commissioned to work on a special project for Hattie too.

"Ms. Hattie, today is the bluebonnet parade in Downtown Dallas. It is going to be beautiful. Are you excited?"

Hattie told Shelia that she just wanted to ride on the truck, not be a part of a parade. She didn't like people fussing over her.

"Well, Ms. Hattie, it's too late!"

Within a few minutes, there was a knock at the door. "They're here!" squealed Shelia. Smiling, Hattie's eyes sparkled as she realized that she had one more thing on her list, well, two really.

"Your chariot awaits you, my dear."

Hattie looked up and gave the biggest grin when she saw Captain Floyd Welding standing at her front door. "My lord a mercy man, what are you doing here? I hadn't seen you in years. You know, I still think you and Helen could have worked things out."

Captain Welding gave a boyish grin as Hattie patted him on his cheek. "All right, Ms. Hattie, today is your day. Maybe you can put in a good word for me with Brown Sugar later."

"You still call her Brown Skin and Brown Sugar. Keep hope alive, son, keep." Captain Welding smiled as he noticed a crowd gathering outside of Hattie's door. Hattie looked surprised as she saw the small crowd lined along her driveway. "Shelia, you didn't tell me that all this was going on."

To her surprise several local ministers stood with their congregations. Alongside the driveway were so many people that she did not recognize. Some were only teenagers at the time she introduced them to Jesus and her peach cobbler. Now they had become ministers, teachers, lawyers, chefs, and doctors. They clapped and cheered as she strode past them. The local Cub Scout troop gave her a salute as if she were in the military. She did consider herself in the Lord's army. Finally, at the end of the line stood the gospel choir from her church singing a rousing version of "I'm a Soldier in the Army of the Lord." Pastor Thompson stepped out, bent down, and gave Hattie a big kiss. She couldn't help but notice that he had on black skinny jeans and a red T-shirt. "Lord have mercy." She laughed. All she visualized was Pastor Thompson preaching her funeral in those same tight skinny jeans. She chuckled with her hand over her mouth. Without warning, Captain Wielding bent down and picked Hattie up as if she were a sack of potatoes. "Let's go, Queen."

"Can we catch a ride?" asked Helen and Secret. With sirens blaring, the fire truck driver slowly drove downtown to get to the back of the line.

Helen and Secret gave their "Miss America" wave and blew kisses to the crowd. Neither had ridden on top of a fire truck before.

"We can see everything from here!" squealed Hattie.

Just then, Captain Welding yelled, "Everybody, here's some candy to throw to the children!"

"That's wonderful." Hattie reached in with both hands and grabbed a handful of candies. Due to her hands shaking, she dropped it.

Secret bent down and grabbed the candies. Rising up, she bumped her head on Hattie's wheelchair. "Ouch," she said, rubbing her head and looking around. Her jaw dropped as she thought, *That's Mercy.* She looked away, not believing her own eyes. *But what is she doing here?* Although the fire truck kept moving, Secret's eyes were glued to the toddler. Looking at her from head to toe, Secret could see that she was dressed really nice and looked clean. Her stroller appeared to be top of the line, but she could see that Mercy had tearstained cheeks. Mercy waved her hand at all the parade floats but wasn't even looking where she was waving. *Her head is down*, thought Secret. Secret threw candies at Picket and hit her in the arm. Picket rubbed her arm and then quickly looked away. What was she doing in town? Mercy's mother looked thin and somewhat pale. *I bet she's back on those drugs. Got my baby over there while she is using!* thought Secret to herself.

"Hey, throw the candy out." Helen had to nudge her daughter to get her attention.

"Oh, I'm sorry. I was just daydreaming, I guess. Granny, are you all right?"

"Oh, baby, I'm fine. This is the best day of my life." Hattie rubbed Secret's hand and kissed it softly.

Secret glanced back at the crowd, but the two people that she knew had disappeared. *I need to focus on Granny right now, but I'm going to get to the bottom of this.*

In June, Texas was hot, gossip was strong, and nearly everyone's temper was as hot as the Texas heat. The morning shift of nurses gathered together in the break room before their shift.

"Good lord, it is hot in here," said Nurse Lisa while fanning herself with a piece of paper. "I should have called in this morning. Y'all know I'm going through the change."

"Hey, Elaine, do you have any hot gossip to share this morning? Was there any action last night?"

"You mean in Mr. Storm's room? No, girl, he actually had a drama-free night. Y'all get all the action on the day shift," she said, sipping her coffee.

"I was off the last few days. Did Mr. Storm have any visitors while I was out?" asked Nurse Janice, brushing off her outfit.

Nurse Rachel and Gina were trying to catch up on the latest gossip. All the female nurses had been talking about how Royce was having two visitors each. "Girl, I hate I missed all the drama," said Janice. Rachel told her that there was no drama because the two women kept missing each other. One was his fiancée, Secret, and the other was his baby's mother, Picket Jones.

Everyone had heard about the fight they had a few months ago. "Child, I just sip my coffee and try to act like I'm working when Picket comes. Isn't her last name Jones?"

"Good morning, ladies, I know you have plenty of work to do this morning," said the charge nurse, Fred. "Get out of that man's business."

Royce had been in his own room for a few weeks. It was obvious that he was getting stronger by the day. His therapy was intensive, and he seemed to be responding well. The nursing staff, especially the female staff, was more than willing to help. He was a well-known figure even in Dallas. The kitchen staff would ask for cooking tips when they brought in his tray. Several employees had his book. It appeared that he was going to have a good recovery, at least mentally. Royce lay back in his bed after a vigorous therapy session. There was a soft knock, then his door squeaked open. "Hello, again," said Picket upon entering his room.

"Again?" Royce appeared confused as he heard a voice but didn't see anyone behind the door.

"Royce, it's me, Picket."

Royce seemed surprised to see Picket although she had been coming to see him for almost a week.

"I needed to talk to you. I've actually been practicing what I wanted to say all week."

Royce looked as if he had seen a ghost. "You look good, Pic."

"You haven't called me that in years," she said, pulling up a seat beside his bed. "Do you mind if I sit down?"

"Not really," said Royce, still stunned.

"I can tell that you are surprised to see me. But I need to tell you that I have been coming all week, but you are always sleeping." He asked her if she had seen their daughter. "Well, I actually have her."

"What do you mean you have her?" Royce appeared agitated. Picket told him that she had taken Mercy back to Jefferson a few weeks ago. He had just assumed that Secret had been keeping Mercy. Secret hadn't told him any different. Royce put both hands on his head in frustration. "Picket, how could you? After all you did last year?"

She stood up from her chair and walked to the window. Looking out, she asked, "Can't you tell I've changed?" Turning back at Royce, she waited for his answer.

He had no comment.

"I am ashamed of what I did last year and the years before that," she said, wiping her eyes, "but I have really changed." Picket told Royce all about her meeting with the chaplain in jail and her wanting to be a good mother for Mercy.

"That brings me to why I am actually here," she said, walking back over to his bed. "Royce, I came to ask for forgiveness from you. I also want to tell you that I forgive you for what you did."

Royce frowned, and he appeared flustered. "What did I do to you?"

Picket bent over and placed both hands on her forehead. "Do you really want to ask that question as if you didn't know?"

Royce asked her again, "What did I do to you? You are the one who took my baby to drug houses, tried to sell her for drugs, and then you had the nerve to abandon our eight-month-old at the bed-and-breakfast. I wasn't even there when you just dumped her like a piece of trash. Anything could have happened to her. To make matters worse, you came back a few months later and kidnapped her from me. I was the one taking loving care of her."

Picket interrupted, "You weren't taking care of nobody." Picket never told anyone, but on the day that she left Mercy, she waited long enough to see if anyone would come out of the bed-and-breakfast. She thought the baby's father was there but wasn't sure. She observed a woman come out of the door and look around. Later, she figured out that Secret was the woman.

"You know good and well that your girlfriend or whatever took care of Mercy."

"How do you know that I didn't?" asked Royce while on the defensive.

Picket huffed, "Because on the day that I kidnapped Mercy, I noticed that she had little bows in her hair. You ain't put cute bows in nobody's hair, did you?"

"Okay, I wasn't up to taking care of anyone at the time. I wasn't even taking care of myself, to be honest. But you just admitted that you kidnapped Mercy from me?"

"Yes, I admit it. I was coming down from meth, and I did anything and everything," she said.

Picket became blurry eyed as she could recall the events of last year so clearly. She sat back and folded her fingers due to Royce continuing his rambling. "I can't believe you would say that you forgive me." It was obvious that the recovering man was becoming angry. "How did you even get out of jail?" asked Royce. "Isn't that what you do? In and out of jail? That's what you do."

"Calm down, Royce! I didn't come here to upset you. I been coming all week to get the courage to talk to you."

"You know I have a head injury, so why are you bringing all this stuff up now? I'm still in the hospital, and you even tell me that you've taken my daughter again." Royce's hands began to sweat, and his heart began to race.

"I told you to calm down. I can assure you that Mercy is being taken care of," said Picket while reaching for his hand.

Royce pulled his hand back and folded his arms. "So is that all you want to say?" he asked sarcastically.

"No, Royce, I need to get something off my chest. I've carried a huge weight around for a long time. And yes, I blamed you for my drug use for a long time." Leaning back in her chair, she said, "Because you weren't there for me, I made a terrible mistake."

Rolling his eyes, he said, "Oh lord, not this again."

"Yes, it's that again. Every time that I bring this up, you won't talk about it. Well, I don't have a lot of time, so I need to forgive you," she said. "Are you on the run from the law or something?"

"Well, forgive me then, and get out."

Picket became visibly upset but pulled out her cell phone and started playing games. Royce asked her why she was playing games on her phone all of a sudden. "Well, I am getting upset, and I can see that you are getting upset, so I am trying to take a break."

"Is that something you learned in rehab?" he asked mockingly.

"Actually, it is. No thanks to you."

"I have to use the restroom," said Royce, turning back his covers. Picket asked him if he needed help.

"Not from you. The only thing that I need from you is my daughter. Can you bring her back?"

"You are still in the hospital, so no, I can't."

Royce told Picket that Secret had been a better mother to Mercy than she could ever be. Royce knew that his words were hurtful, but he said them anyway. He may not have admitted it, but he was bitter against this baby's mother. She also had bitterness and regret in her heart.

"Royce, I can't believe that you would ever say that to me. Well, just so you know, your girlfriend is not her mother and never will be."

Royce tried to stand up by himself, but he was still unstable without his walker. Falling back, he looked at Picket with some embarrassment. Again, he tried to stand by himself but fell into Picket's arms. He didn't want to admit it, but Picket looked lovely. Her face was glowing even though she looked slightly pale. Wrapping her arms around his neck, Picket gave a grin. "See, you're doing all that smart talking and still can't stand up straight." His muscle arms leaned over Picket as he tried to push himself back in bed. "It's okay. I got you, baby daddy."

"Well, I wish I wasn't."

"Yes, but you are."

"I'm still mad at you for taking my child," said Royce. "I could use a little help, though."

"Put your hands around my waist and pull yourself up. I'm little, but I'm tough," she said. Just as Royce put his hands around her waist, he fell back onto the bed. Picket lost her footing and fell on top of Royce. Both laughed due to bumping their heads together.

Just then, both looked up due to the room door slamming. It was Secret, Royce's bride-to-be, and she was already pulling off her earrings and pulling her hair back into a ponytail. "I knew it! That was you I saw at the parade. And to think I just came from a prayer meeting, and look, the devil is in the room."

Picket rolled her eyes and gave a sigh.

"Lord, help me to get this devil out of here." With that being said, Secret began to slowly walk toward Picket with both of her fists clenched. She intended to end this visitation, and she meant for good. "Get off of him!"

"Fred, you need to get in there!" said Janice while waving her arms. She was trying to talk quietly, but it was not working due to her being in a patient's room.

"What? Get your in where?" he asked.

"I'll be right back, Mr. Chase," said Janice. Janice walked quickly over to Fred and pointed toward Royce's room. "The fiancée is here!"

"So?" Fred shrugged his shoulders while continuing to chart his work.

"Did you see the baby momma come in earlier?" Fred looked as if he did not know what Janice was talking about. "Fred, let me spell it out for you! The baby's momma is in the room that the fiancée just walked into. Remember the fight months ago and how they almost tore up the room," Janice whispered while making large arm gestures. "Do you get it now?"

"Oh," said Fred as if a light bulb went off. "Excuse me please." Fred walked hastily down to Royce's room to hopefully avoid World War III.

Royce had been recovering nicely from his traumatic brain injury, but he did not need the added stress that was going on.

"What are you doing here, Picket?" asked Secret as she stood behind the lady who was lying on top of Royce.

"It's not what it looks like. Or is it?" Picket puckered toward Royce's face.

Secret's mouth flew open, and she said, "Oh no you didn't."

Royce interrupted with one finger raised. "Pic, stop it!" he said, pushing her off him. "Babe, it really is not what it looks like. There is nothing going on here."

"Since you can't seem to understand that I need you to leave my fiancé alone, I need to help you."

Picket looked at Secret and said, "I thought you just came from a prayer meeting."

"I did, but it hasn't kicked in yet."

With that being said, Secret leaped onto Picket's back and began pulling her ponytail. It was indeed a sight as Picket pushed herself against the wall. The push caused Secret to hit her back on the hard surface. Secret punched Picket in her lip before falling onto the chair beside Royce's bed.

"Oh, I can't breathe. My god," said Royce, grabbing his chest.

Secret lost her focus and grabbed Royce. "Babe, I'm so sorry. Babe . . ." The bride grabbed Royce in her arms. She leaned close to his face to listen to his breathing.

With a smile, he said, "Now that's what I'm talking about."

Secret hit him on the shoulder. "Man, there isn't anything wrong with you. You should be ashamed of yourself, scaring me that way."

Fred swung the door open. With both hands up in the air, he said, "All right, ladies, let's settle down. This is a hospital, so get out of here."

Secret sat up and pointed at the woman who seemed to be a thorn in her side. Looking at the charge nurse, she said, "Fred, we all know that you ain't gone do nothing. Besides, there is no problem here." Looking at Picket, Secret asked, "Miss Thing, is there a problem here?"

"Um, no," she said while walking quickly outside the room.

"Royce, is there a problem here?" asked Secret to her fiancé while giving him a piercing stare.

Royce looked at her and threw both his hands up. Clearing his throat, he said, "There's no problem here."

"All right, Nurse Fred, you can go on and let me visit my fiancé," she said, shooing him out the door.

"Babe, did you really just come from a prayer meeting?"

"Yes, I really did, but I think it needed more time to kick in."

"No, it didn't. Looks like you needed to stay until God finished the job," said Royce, chuckling! "Help, Lord."

"I am trying, but that woman just drains all the Jesus right out of me." Secret poured Royce a glass of water and sat beside his bed. "What was she doing here anyway?" she asked while looking at all of Royce's monitor numbers.

"Well, she came to ask me to forgive her and likewise."

"What?"

Royce told Secret about the conversation between him and Picket before she came through the door. "She really did fall on me, and there was nothing else going on."

Although Secret believed him, she gave him a side lip. "Um hum."

Royce continued, "She always wants to talk to me about what happened between us, but I don't."

Secret pushed the nurse call button. "Yes, could I have a cup of coffee?"

"Sure, Ms. Bell, I will bring it right in."

"Yes, and please bring my vanilla cream this time. Because the last time, you did not. Thank you."

"Stop giving them folks a tough time," said Royce. "This is not Starbucks."

"I'm going to give you a hard time, if you don't tell me what happened between you two."

Just then, a knock came on the door. "Here you are, Ms. Bell," said Fred with a fake smile on his face.

"The charge nurse doesn't bring in coffee, Fred."

"I know, but I had to make sure that you had no more complaints or orders at this time." Fred rolled his eyes and walked out of the room. Both Royce and Secret laughed.

"Since I know this is going to be a long story, I thought I should get comfortable," she said, taking a sip.

"All right, mister, start talking."

Chapter 14

His Side, Her Side, the Truth

Picket and Royce were inseparable in high school. The young lovers talked about going to college together then getting married. "We can get through anything if we stick together," said Royce while he held Picket's hand. They went to Sam Houston State University as a couple. Picket James was described as beautiful; she was described as drop-dead gorgeous. It didn't hurt that she was incredibly smart and was at the top of her class in high school and college. With a major in architecture, she was showing signs of much promise in the wide-open field. As a black woman, she would be nearly in a class all by herself. Royce, her boyfriend, was a star football player; and every scout in the state of Texas had followed him from high school to Sam Houston State. It was almost certain that he was going to join the pros really soon.

Their desire for each other outweighed their passion for their individual futures. They studied together, ate together, and spent nearly every waking moment together. Royce and Picket had a strong bond with each other, sometimes a bit too strong. "Royce, I need to talk to you."

Royce could see that his girlfriend looked somewhat flustered. With a kiss, he said, "Okay, we can talk right after football practice."

"I got some good news for you too, babe. We have to celebrate."

Picket went back to her dorm and lay down. She had been feeling sick lately and had trouble concentrating on her schoolwork. The junior in college had such a bright future, but the future was interrupted by a positive pregnancy test.

Royce picked his girlfriend up and took her to Chili's. Picket usually ate her chicken salad; but she had ribs, salad, tea, and bread.

"Babe, you are eating up a storm," said Royce while wiping Picket's face. "Don't think I haven't noticed that big old booty. But it does look good on you." Royce was just kidding, but Picket began to cry.

"Come on, Pic, I was just playing."

"Royce, I'm pregnant!"

Royce looked around the restaurant to see if anyone else had heard her. Of course, several people did because she screamed it out while sobbing loudly.

Royce just kept eating while handing the crying young woman a piece of tissue.

Picket looked at Royce with disbelief. "Did you hear what I said? I am pregnant."

"How far?" asked Royce while wiping barbecue sauce off his fingers.

"About six weeks, I think."

"So what did your parents say?" asked Royce, now looking up at his girlfriend.

"I don't know because I haven't told them yet. I figured, since you're the father, you should be the first to know." Picket put her face in both of her hands and began to weep heavily. Royce put his hand on top of hers. Then he moved over to her bench and sat beside her. He held her close to his side.

"What are you going to do? I mean I have my football scholarship. I'm going to the pros." Royce told her that his big news was that several pro football teams were interested in him. He was considering entering the NFL draft at the end of his senior year. He'd graduate with a degree in kinesiology and go to the pros. "Mom said I need something to fall back on in case I get injured." Picket looked upside Royce's head due to him going on and on about his future that didn't seem to include her.

Picket stopped crying and said, "Royce Storm, I just told you that we are having a baby and you are talking like I haven't said anything."

"You're going to be an architect, and we don't have any room for a baby," said Royce.

Picket wiped her eyes and blew her nose. "What do you mean we don't have room for a baby? I'm pregnant, so we better make time."

"Listen, Pic, since neither one of us are ready to be parents, we need to see if there are other options."

"Royce do you want to put the baby up for adoption?"

"No, I wasn't thinking that," he said.

"Well, what were you talking about? I don't have other options right now. Either we keep the baby or we give it up for adoption." Picket was obviously becoming frustrated with Royce's tone. She wasn't sure what she'd thought he say, but she didn't expect the conversation to go like this.

"Pic, it's still early, and you still have time to have an abortion."

"A what?" Picket couldn't believe that the man that she loved was suggesting ending her pregnancy. "Why would you even suggest that? You told me that we could get through anything together. You said you'd be there when I needed you." Picket's voice was getting louder and louder.

"Babe, calm down," he said, trying to quiet her. "Look, nobody has to know. I'm just saying I can't have a baby slowing me down." Royce began to rub his hands on his pants leg. "I am so close to the pros. We can have everything we dreamed of, babe."

Picket's sorrow turned to anger. "Royce Storm, are you serious right now?"

"Pic, we've been together since high school, but I can't let anything stand in the way of my dreams. Not even you or a baby."

"So are you saying you're not going to be here with me?"

How could the man that she loved tell her he didn't want to be a father? Of course she wanted to be a mother one day, but it's not like she was happy about the baby either. Even with all of that, she hadn't thought about ending her pregnancy. In a passing moment, she thought about how cute the baby would be.

"Maybe my parents will help me? They could keep the baby while we are at school. Maybe I could go to night school to finish my degree." Picket tried to convince the reluctant father that maybe they could work it out. Nothing worked to convince Royce that anything would work except ending the pregnancy.

In just two more years she would graduate with a degree in architecture. "Royce, I am going to be making enough money to take care of a baby," she said in one more desperate attempt.

"But, you aren't making any money right now."

"You know I come from money and I think my parents will support us in the meantime."

"Yes, but will they? You haven't even asked them. I don't want to talk about this now. I'm going back to my dorm room alone. I'll tell you what, if your parents agree to help, I may consider it. If they won't, then you know what you need to do."

Picket tried to get up enough nerve to call her parents. She couldn't believe that Royce had abandoned her in every way possible. This was a major issue, and he made it clear that he was not going to be there for her. Not only that, but he didn't even consider putting the baby up for adoption. Picket decided to go home for the weekend and talk to her parents.

"What's the matter, baby?" asked Mrs. Jones. "You sounded really upset on the phone."

"Mom, I'm pregnant." She wasn't sure what response her mother would give besides disappointment. Mrs. Jones sat back on her recliner and pulled out her cell phone.

"Mom, did you hear what I just said?"

"Yes, I did."

"Well, aren't you going to say anything?" asked Picket, looking at her mother.

Mrs. Jones pulled off her reading glasses and went and sat beside her daughter. "Picket, you are almost finished with college with a promising career. What were you thinking? You didn't even protect yourself or your future!"

Crying, Picket said, "Royce doesn't even want to be a father. He told me to basically end the pregnancy. Can you believe him?"

Mrs. Jones was not a bit shocked due to hearing that he didn't want the baby. "Daughter, I love you, but I think Royce is right, this time. You can't have a baby right now."

Picket wiped her tears. "But can you and Daddy help out? I've thought of going to night school. I'll be making good money after I graduate." To her disappointment, Picket's mother told her that she could not support her decision to have the baby.

"That's what I was looking for on my cell. You're still early, so it should be pretty simple, shouldn't it?" Why was Picket the only one who wanted to keep her baby? She had never been in this position before, but she really felt like she could make this work. Part of her wanted to be a mother, although she didn't want to be one now. Was everyone right?

"I'm going to bed, Mom."

"Okay, but I'm taking you down to the clinic in the morning. We are going to take care of this, okay?" Mrs. Jones never told Mr. Jones that her daughter was pregnant.

The next morning, Picket went through with terminating her pregnancy. Picket told Royce what happened, and he seemed relieved that he was no longer a father. His future was certain, and he and Picket would resume their lives as if nothing ever happened.

Secret sipped her coffee as Royce told her about his and Picket's past. Shaking her head, Secret said, "Royce, you were so wrong, and that's a lot coming from me. Even I can't believe that you did that to Picket." Royce frowned because he couldn't believe that Secret was taking Picket's side. He explained to her that he was not prepared to be a father, and he thought that was best for them.

"Is that what she wanted to talk to you about?"

"Yes, but I don't want to."

Secret shook her head and grabbed her fiancé's hand. "Royce Storm, it's seems like you made the best decision for you, not Picket. How could you leave her alone like that to make a serious decision?"

In all these years, he had never thought about how Picket felt. He just thought she had moved on just like he had.

"Royce, you need to apologize to that woman," said Secret, picking up her phone.

"Maybe later."

Secret hit Royce on his shoulder and said, "No, sir, you need to call her right now. Can't you see she is still in pain from that? You wouldn't listen then, but I'm going to make sure that you listen now."

"My arm is hurting," he said while rubbing his shoulder.

"Well, give me the number and I'll dial. Call her back up here, now!"

Secret dialed the number and quickly handed the phone to Royce. Royce turned his head and pushed the phone away. "You better take this phone right now or I promise I'll—" said Secret, gritting her teeth.

A voice could be heard coming from the phone, "Hello! Who's there? Hello."

"Uh, hi, Pic, this is Royce," he said grudgingly. "I know you're surprised to hear from me, but can you come up to the hospital?"

"Now?" asked Picket, talking loudly.

"Yes, now. I already know you're still in town. By the way, did you bring my daughter? Where is she?" asked Royce.

Secret snatched the phone and hung up due to the conversation turning into another direction. "Royce, we are not talking about Mercy. I am upset too, but let's focus on this apology first. I'm working on finding out where Mercy is."

"Okay, babe, I'm going to be cool. First things first. Can I get some lunch?" asked Royce while he pushed the nurse call button. After a mediocre lunch, the hospital room door creaked open.

Picket looked around the room as if she expected trouble. Before she could say anything, she heard Secret's voice, "Yes, I am still here. Just in case you were wondering."

Picket saw Secret sitting in a chair next to Royce. Picket guardingly sat on the other side of the hospital room while keeping her eyes on Royce and Secret. With both eyebrows raised, Picket asked, "What's going on?"

"Ms. Jones, I'm not going to hurt you. You can relax. I actually hope that you two can talk."

"What? You don't even want me near Royce," said Picket with her defenses up.

"You got that right, and I still don't want you near him, but this is important."

"Royce, if you two think you're gonna gang up on me, then

you have another thing coming." Secret interrupted, raising her hand toward Picket, "Sassy girl, ain't nobody trying to do nothing to you." Secret leaned over and planted a big passionate kiss on her fiancé so that Picket could see it. She also made sure that Picket could see her beautiful diamond engagement ring. "Babe, I hate to rush, but I need to go check your mail in Tyler." Picket just rolled her eyes and sat back in her seat with both arms folded. "Miss Thing, I will be back, so don't try anything with my fiancé while I'm gone either."

Royce asked Picket to come sit close to him on the bed. Instead of anger and disappointment, he had a certain tenderness in his look toward her. "Pic, you've wanted to talk to me for a long time, so go ahead on and talk. I really am listening to you this time." Picket didn't know what to think about anything that Royce had said so far. First he called her out of the blue, then the woman who hated her left the room. What was going on? Part of her felt suspicious, but part was hoping that the man she once loved was telling the truth.

Although Picket's mind had wandered, Royce kept talking. "And I want to tell you that I'm sorry for the times I didn't listen. I knew you wanted to talk about what happened, but I didn't. The first time you blamed me for your drug use, I just exploded." Picket remembered that Royce had become enraged the first time he caught her using drugs. She blamed him for her use but didn't tell him why. "I still don't understand why do you blamed me for getting on drugs. What was it?"

Picket slowly moved off the bed and sat in a chair where Secret had been sitting. She began to pull out some tissue from her purse. "Royce, it was the guilt of what I had done."

"What do you mean?"

"You see, I never wanted to end my pregnancy. I was forced by my mother to go to the clinic the weekend after I told you about the baby. Some women seem to go on with life after an abortion, but I got stuck because I never wanted to have one."

Royce sat up in bed and leaned forward with full attention. He thought he knew everything about his ex-girlfriend, but this was new information. The box of tissues was soon empty due to Picket being choked by her tears. She continued to blubber and tell the rest of the story. "I should have been brave and strong. Maybe I should have run away. Weeks after I done it, I realized that there was so many things I could have done." Picket admitted that guilt and shame had eaten her up for many years. "Royce, I told you that I ended the pregnancy on that day, but I never told you what really happened. "

"Okay, so tell me now."

"Well, you already know how you acted," she said, looking at him side-eyed. Indeed, he recalled how he acted, and he held his head down. "I couldn't believe that you told me you would not be there for me. We had planned to get married, and we were going to be parents one day. Just sooner than what we had planned. I wasn't racing to be a mom either, but I realized we were in that situation. Something inside of me desired to be the mother that I knew I could be." Royce folded his arms and turned his lips to the side, mainly because he knew she was telling the truth. "And then you told me that nothing was going to get in the way of your dreams of going to the NFL. I couldn't believe you were being so selfish." Although it had been years ago, Picket still had strong feelings about the ordeal.

Royce knew that he had been incredibly selfish. He had nearly become obsessed with going to the NFL. Only a few months later, he had a leg injury that ruined all his chances. It was uncomfortable to hear a hard truth, but it was necessary. "Well, go head-on and finish," said Royce.

"I told my mom that I was pregnant and thought she'd be supportive. Mom said that you were right and that I didn't have room for a baby."

Royce rolled his eyes at Picket because she reached for a second box of tissue. How could he comfort a woman whom he almost hated? Picket walked toward the window and turned her back on Royce.

"I felt hopeless because my mother didn't even give me a chance to talk or say anything. What's so bad about a baby? I thought. I just wasn't strong enough to even tell her I could make it without you or my family." She turned around and looked at Royce who was now on the defensive. "I wasn't sure if I could take care of a baby with no support from you or my parents. What was I going to do still two years away from graduating? So the next morning, my mother took me to the clinic, and I literally got out the car and ran as fast as I could down the street. I could not go through with it. I cried and cried. Somehow my mother found me and forced me back in the car. She told me that if I did not go through with this, she would never have anything else to do with me. Her and my father would no longer pay for my college. I wouldn't get a job, and she would take my car."

"That must have really been scary for you."

Turning back to the bed, Picket said, "I had nobody, and so she pushed me in there, and I went through with it. I was in so much pain, and I cried and cried." Royce asked her to come over to him. Picket took several deep breaths and blew her nose.

"Is that what caused you to use drugs?" asked Royce with much curiosity.

"No, Royce, even all that didn't cause me to use drugs. I was depressed, but I wasn't a drug addict. Two weeks later, I went into the gas station close to the campus. I ran into this lady inside the restroom. She was crying uncontrollably and shaking. I wanted to reach out to her, but everything in me was still so broken. I tried to walk out quickly, but she reached out and grabbed my hand. The lady told me that she had had a miscarriage about four months earlier, and she was still devastated. She asked me if I knew anyone who wanted to put a baby up for adoption. What made matters worse was that she had just been told that she could never have kids again. The lady was on her way to have a total hysterectomy."

Royce just shook his head because this story was getting worse and worse. The pain in Picket's voice was so thick, it seemed like a knife could cut it.

"I literally could not believe that I had just ended the baby's life and here this lady was with a bleeding heart. I could have given her my baby!" she cried. The only thing Royce knew was to grab Picket's hand. She was becoming hysterical while telling the story.

Picket continued, "She was a good person, and my baby could have gone to a good family. If only I'd waited just a few weeks. I realized there were people around who were willing to help me, but I didn't find out until it was too late. I couldn't deal with it, so I ran out of the gas station. The next thing I knew, I was trying cocaine so that I could numb the pain of my mistake.

"After that, I know we broke up. Besides that one night we hooked up some years later, I never wanted to see you again. I felt that you were a constant reminder of my life going down the tubes." A slight smile came across Picket's face as she squeezed Royce's hand. "At least we got Mercy out of that one night." Royce smiled as well thinking of how much he loved his little girl. "The crazy thing is that I had wanted to be a mother all those years, but I was so messed up by the time I finally became one. I felt like a train going out of control, and I could not forgive myself or you, for that matter."

After Royce finally listened to every word that came out of Picket's mouth, he felt stunned. He played with his hands and looked away all to avoid crying himself. Mostly because it was true; he did cause her much pain and grief that could have been avoided. Where would she have been if he had been there for her?

"Hey, did you hear what I just said?" asked Picket, snapping her fingers at Royce. He had been daydreaming while she was talking. "I said that when I met Jesus, I realized that I had to forgive myself and you. I wanted to tell you that I truly forgive you and let you go." There was a sweet smile that came across Picket's face. The light of hope was truly shining on her skin. Royce held his head down.

"Pic, I ask you to forgive me. I was so wrong to leave you in that position. I was stupid and selfish. You're right, I broke a promise to you because I wasn't there when you needed me. I never even told my parents because I knew better." Picket and Royce talked for a couple of hours; and for the first time, in years, they really listened to each other. "Help me get up," said Royce.

"Why?"

"Because I have something to do."

Picket didn't know what Royce was going to do. She helped him and then handed him his walker so that he could have something to hold on to. Royce went and opened the hospital window. Then he asked Picket to take a seat. Leaning out the window, he shouted, "To every woman on behalf of every man, I am sorry! Picket Jones, I was wrong, and I am sorry!"

"Royce, stop it. You don't have to do that. Don't hurt yourself. If you die, your crazy fiancée is going to kill me, and I can't fight that woman again."

Royce hobbled over to the hallway and yelled out, "I, Royce Storm, apologizes because I told Picket Jones that I would be there; but I left her alone to figure it out! Picket Jones, I am sorry for putting you in a bad position. I messed up!" Royce raised up his arms in a dramatic fashion.

Picket put her hand over her face and sank down in her chair. She was embarrassed but couldn't help but laugh a little at the loud display.

"Mr. Storm, please go lay down! Go back to your room carrying on," said the charge nurse, walking quickly to his room. "You are making a scene. Please, stop it."

"Fred, I owe this beautiful woman an apology. This is my baby's mother, and I have not been there at any time that she needed me."

"All right, brother, it's going to be okay. Just don't get your pressure all up." Fred helped Royce get back to his hospital bed.

"Well, Picket, do you forgive me?" asked Royce, holding out his hand. Picket told him that there was no way she could disregard that kind of apology. "Okay, I just wanted you to know how sorry I truly am."

Picket became real serious while grabbing Royce's hand. "There is another reason that I have been coming up here, but I will talk to you about that later," she said. "Do you mind if we pray together? It wouldn't hurt if we both talked to God about this whole situation and truly put it behind us." Royce agreed because he had never asked God to forgive him for playing a part in the death of his unborn child. He had never felt sorry for what he had done. For the first time in their entire lives, they prayed together as parents.

"I think that's enough for today," said Fred. He had been standing in the door through the entire prayer. "Man, that was truly a blessing, and it made me think of what I need to do later."

"Really?" asked Royce.

"Yeah, man, I got a few women that I need to apologize to. I'm not going to even lie."

"Well, Mr. Fred, I am glad that our drama helped someone else, I guess." Picket left the hospital feeling relieved, free, and closer to God. Royce thought about their conversation for the rest of the evening. He didn't feel sad; he felt free. Placing his arms behind his head, he drifted off to a peaceful sleep.

Chapter 15

Complicated Matters

Secret had a hot but pleasant ride to Tyler, Texas. Her car air-conditioning barely kept up with the June Texas heat. She had to pull over once due to her car overheating. "You old pile of junk. I'm trading you off as soon as I can." She needed to trade in her red Ford Explorer but was trying to save money for her and Royce's future. The Secret Place Restaurant was all but closed, and Royce had run through all the money his parents had left him. With his book sales dismal, she felt that she had to save money for their future.

The mailbox was full of disconnection notices and a few letters from his pen pal, Davis. "Oh shoot," said Secret while stuffing the mail in her purse. Secret had not thought about the utilities being turned off. The owner of the house had been in the hospital for a few months, and no bills had been paid at his home. "Goodness gracious, it's hot in here!" Secret felt like she was in a sauna upon opening the door. Flicking on the lights, she said, "Well, I know I'm not staying long in here."

Secret briefly looked around to make sure that everything was still in place. Her lips turned downward as she noticed a few of Mercy's toys still in the corner. She had a little recliner right beside her father's. "Snap out of it, girl."

Taking time to cool off, she sat in the Ford and read through each and every letter. Galaxy Bank had written Royce a letter with all types of red stickers on it. "Oh man, they done took the restaurant."

Mr. Storm, this letter is to inform you that the Secret Place has now been foreclosed due to lack of payment. We are putting it up for auction in October. Please contact Galaxy Bank for any further questions.

I'm sure the employees already know that they have no job by now, Secret thought. Driving by the restaurant, she could see the chains on the front of the doors. "That's a real shame," she said, wiping her tears away. Royce had named the restaurant after her as a token of his love toward her. Now it was closed for good. Although she hated to leave things in a mess, she was helpless to do anything about it. Like a roller coaster malfunctioning, her plans had been derailed.

She decided to change her focus and read Davis's letter. *I wonder what Mr. Davis Patton is up to.* She was used to reading all Royce's mail for now. "Royce, I haven't heard from you in a long time. What's up?" Davis was letting his pen pal know that he would be at the wedding in August. "Dude, I got some news for you! My stepfather sent me a stack of letters that he found in my mom's closet. I'm still digging for more information about my past." Royce had never sent the address of the church, so he was asking for a return letter. Secret put the letter back in its envelope and sighed. *Sorry, Davis, I hate to tell you the wedding is going to be cancelled for now.* Secret knew that Royce wasn't up for writing any letters right now, but she planned to write Davis back later.

Secret dreaded the nearly two-hour drive back to Dallas. All she could think about was all that was going on. She had used up all of her paid family medical leave. Now she was not getting paid although her job was still being held for her. She had to cancel the summer wedding, the restaurant had been foreclosed upon, Mercy's location was still unknown, and she didn't have enough money to support her, Royce, and maybe two children.

Secret had told her mother that they were just going to put the wedding on hold for a while. They understood that Royce needed more time to recover. "I hope Granny isn't too disappointed," said Secret, cringing. She had only driven a few miles out of Tyler, but due to her racing thoughts, she pulled over in a small town called Athens. "Hello," said Secret, answering her cell phone.

"Hello, Ms. Bell, this is Dr. Raven. How are you today?"

"Oh, fine, Doctor, is everything okay?" Secret knew that usually doctors did not call themselves.

"Yes, Ms. Bell. I just wanted to tell you that Mr. Storm is on schedule to be released in a few weeks."

Secret smiled due to the good news. At least something positive was going on. "That's the best news I've heard all day."

"We feel that he's reached his full potential in the hospital. However, he's got to continue therapy at the David Conner inpatient rehab center so that he can fully return back to normal."

"How long will he have to be there?"

"At least thirty to sixty days, if all goes well. He does have a long road ahead, but I am confident that Mr. Storm will have a full recovery."

As a nurse practitioner, Secret knew that a lot of people with head injuries never returned to normal.

"Doctor, you know I'll do my best, and I'll make sure that he attends all his therapy appointments."

"Ms. Bell, I know this is off the subject, but I called for another reason also. I heard you are one of the best nurse practitioners in Dallas. I am considering starting a private practice and would love to have you on our team. You're more than qualified, and I would love to oversee you as the attending physician."

Secret was surprised. Was this an answered prayer? Her income would increase by thousands of dollars. She had considered moving to Tyler with Royce, but he had lost the restaurant anyway. Maybe he could move to Dallas and start over there.

"I'll think about it, Dr. Raven. Thank you so much." Her tears had turned into a smile, and for the first time in a few weeks, she saw a glimmer of hope.

Two weeks later, Royce was all smiles as he was released from the hospital and transferred to an inpatient rehab. The facility was close to Secret's home, and she could have closer contact with him. Helen and Secret agreed to care for Royce at their home after his discharge. There was no way he could return to his Tyler home with no utilities, no income, and no child.

"What are you going to do for the Fourth of July?" asked Shelia to Helen over the phone.

"Not sure, I'll see if Secret wants to do anything," she said.

"Okay, we need to get together and discuss how we are going to get Hattie back to Arkansas for her final bucket list wish."

"Girl, you are sure right. I'll talk to Secret tonight. She went to see Royce at the rehab today."

"Helen, how are you going with your other job that Hattie gave you?"

"Don't worry about my part. How is your part coming?" asked Helen.

Shelia smiled. "I can't wait! Girl, your family has a lot going on."

Helen knew that they did have a lot going on. Not only had Hattie given Secret an assignment to help her fulfill her final wishes, the dying woman also had Helen and Shelia working on a secret wedding gift for Secret. In just a few weeks, Hattie's health had declined quickly. She had lost her ability to walk and now relied totally on oxygen. Shelia had to transfer her from her hospital bed to her wheelchair daily. Although the time of her departure was getting near, Hattie had refused to go to the hospice center. She felt that she ironed the right to die peacefully at the place of her choice. "So far she is hanging in there," said Shelia, talking to Hattie's pastor. Several people came to see her every day and help Shelia when needed. No one wanted to admit it, but she had a few weeks at best, but her spirit was still strong.

Secret gave Royce a kiss on the lips when she saw him doing his therapy. "Good work, babe," she said, giving him a thumbs-up. She would sit quietly and read a magazine while he completed therapy. She wanted to be involved, but he didn't want her to.

"Just watch, Secret, you are not on duty here," he said. He had good days and bad days. His head injury was nearly healed, but he still had issues. Royce was still upset that he would have to use a cane for a while. Some days he was calm, and other days his temper seemed out of control. He would throw things, threaten to walk home, and refuse to eat. Secret had never seen Royce so angry.

The physical therapist said, "Secret, we are pushing him hard because we know he can do it." Being a physician's assistant, she knew that fits of rage and sorrow were common for a traumatic brain injury patient.

"Actually Mr. Storm is doing very well. I can tell that most of his personality has returned. He is using his walker less, but he still had a lot of work to do," said Leroy to the worried bride-to-be. She became tearful while she watched Royce struggle to take painful steps without his walker. Royce had received news that he had no severe internal injuries, although his ribs still needed more time to heal.

A lady approached Secret and sat beside her. Extending her hand, she said, "Ms. Bell, I'm Rachel, one of Mr. Storm's therapists. I realized we're missing a few of his spinal x-rays from the hospital. I thought that we had everything when he was transferred here, but we didn't. Would it be an inconvenience for you to go to Dallas County Hospital and see if they could give you a disc with his x-rays on it?"

"Of course, whatever you need," said Secret.

Deciding to visit the same floor that Royce had been on, Secret smiled seeing the charge nurse. "Hey, Fred, you haven't quit yet," she said, walking toward him.

"Who let you in here? Should we start locking room doors?"

"Fred, don't start nothing up in here," she said. Both of them laughed as he reminded her of all the fights she had at the hospital. "I am truly sorry about all of that, Fred. I know that was truly unprofessional."

Fred told her that it gave them all something to talk about. "Well, I'm just here to pick up some medical records and then I'm going back to the rehab to visit Royce." The nurses all gathered around her to ask how Royce was doing. He had made quite an impression on them and the kitchen staff as well. "Oh, he's doing well. You know how it is. He's taking it one step at a time, but hopefully he'll be home pretty soon."

Fred said, "I hope he will be fine by the time of the wedding in August."

"Well, we were, but we had to cancel the wedding, but just temporarily we're going to aim for next year. Hopefully by that time everything will be a lot better." Secret had no time to go into great detail about all the things that had gone wrong in their lives.

"Hey, Freddie, are you coming? I rang my buzzer like forty times. You heard me!"

Secret recognized the familiar voice coming from a room down the hallway. Fred held his head down. "That woman is really getting on my nerves," he said. "I'm trying to be professional, but Lord have mercy, that is one of the worst patients I've ever had." Fred began looking at his watch. "I'm calling in sick tomorrow. I just can't with this woman."

Secret looked at Fred with a confused look. "Is that who I think it is in there?" Fred whistled and looked upside the wall. "Fred, you hear me."

"Yes, and if anyone should be familiar with that voice, I know you should be," he said, pointing at her while backing away.

"Ms. Jones, what do you need this time?" he asked, pressing the nurse response button.

Fred received news of an emergency in another room, so he walked off. Secret looked both ways to see if anyone was watching as she slowly made her way down to the room where the voice was coming from.

"Freddie, I asked you for more cream in my coffee! Where is the cream?" shouted Picket to the door as it slowly opened.

"Picket, what are you doing here?" Secret was startled as she noticed that the hollering woman had lost at least fifteen pounds since the last time they saw each other a few weeks ago.

Picket looked thin, pale, and fragile. The dark circles around her eyes made her look several years older. Secret rushed over to her bed and leaned into Picket's face. "I knew it. You overdosed, didn't you? How long have you been on drugs? Where is Mercy? Please don't tell me you tried to sell her again." Picket had a coughing fit while being accused by Secret.

Picket held her hand up so that Secret could stop verbally attacking her. "What are you doing here?"

Secret told her that it was none of her business why she was there. "But if you must know, I came to pick up some records for Royce. I just stopped by to give an update to the nurses. Now getting back to you, Miss Thing. Am I right that you overdosed?"

Secret began pacing in the room as she felt herself become angry with Picket. Picket looked at the ceiling as she was accused of using drugs and everything else.

"Secret, you need to shut up for a minute," said Picket, having another coughing fit. There was some paperwork on the patient desk next to the hospital bed. Secret snatched the papers and walked over to the window ceil.

"Give those back. You can't look at my personal information."

"Maybe not, but I'm looking anyway. I am a nurse, you know."

"Yes, but you're not my nurse."

Picket attempted to throw her bed cover off and get out of bed, but she was too weak. She fell back onto the bed.

"Put that down! That is none of your business," she said, almost frantic. Secret gave Picket "the hand" and turned her back. She realized that Picket was not there for an overdose, but she had end-stage liver disease. The paperwork was about hospice and end-of-life care plans. Secret was stunned, embarrassed, and somewhat confused.

Picket cleared her throat and said, "Look, Ms. Nosey, I came here to see if there was anything else they could do for me. I've actually been here in Dallas for a while doing all kinds of tests and taking experimental medication."

Secret listened intensely then asked, "So what did they say?"

"Not that you care, but they said there is nothing else they can try. I'm all out of options and time," she said tearfully.

Secret had no words due to being completely shocked by the conversation. "Is that why you wanted to talk to Royce? To get things right between you two?"

"Yes, I want to make sure that all my bitterness is out of my heart. I want to go to heaven, and I can't go with unforgiveness in my heart."

Secret was somewhat convicted because she had a few people that she needed to forgive, mainly Picket Jones. "Girl, I know you are telling the truth on that. We all got some work to do, don't we?" said Secret, pouring Picket a glass of water.

She quietly pulled up a chair up very close to the bed. She didn't say a word for about ten minutes. Finally, Secret grabbed the deck of cards on Picket's nightstand.

"So, Ms. Jones, what do you know about playing spades?"

"What did you say?" asked Picket on the defensive. She had been staring at the ceiling and trying to ignore her unwanted guest. Secret began to deal and shuffled the cards.

Picket frowned and responded, "You better not be cheating either. I know about playing spades. I am a champion." She shuffled through the cards in her hand.

"Show me what you got, Ms. Jones. I can't beat you up with these hands, but I can whip you up on these cards right here," said Secret with a grin.

Picket gave a slight tearful chuckle while pushing herself up in bed. "I don't know about that. I still got something left for you, Ms. Bell. You don't have on those spike red stilettos, do you? I called those your supershoes. I still can't believe you fought me in those shoes."

"Why?"

"Because every time you wear those, somebody is in trouble," said Picket.

"You know what, Ms. Jones, you got a mean swing yourself. I told Royce that I literally didn't have the strength to fight you anymore. You took me to the streets, girl," said Secret." Both women tried to hold their laughter, but they burst out in a loud giggle at the same time.

"All right, let's play," said Secret. "And no, I didn't wear my supershoes today."

The two women began to play cards for about an hour. They didn't talk about Mercy, Royce, or liver disease. "Are you getting tired?" asked Secret, watching Picket rubbing her chest.

"A little bit, but I'm okay."

The hospital social worker, Latisha, came in with more paperwork. "I'm sorry, Ms. Jones, I didn't know you had company. Would you like me to come back later?"

"No, it's not like I have much time left, so you might as well say whatever you need to say."

Secret grabbed her purse and said, "Oh, that's fine. I can give you two some privacy."

"No, I want you to stay, please," said Picket with desperate eyes. Secret agreed and quietly pulled her chair up to the bed.

Latisha went through the hospice information as Secret held her head down and played with her cell phone. All she could think about was her dying so young and leaving her own toddler without a mother. Secret had misjudged Picket all this time, and she felt guilty for fighting a dying woman. She had also been thinking of her grandmother being in the same situation. How could she handle two women that she knew dying at the same time?

Secret interjected while squeezing the crying woman's hand, "Don't you have any friends who could stay with you?"

"No, when I left the drug scene, I lost all my friends."

Latisha paused and handed Picket a box of tissue. "Do you have any close family that will be able to look after you during this time?" Picket told the social worker that she had no family except a little girl.

Latisha marked an x by family support then said, "I'll have to send you to the hospice center."

"You mean I'll die alone at a hospital? No, I can't, please!" Picket told Latisha that she had money, so she could pay someone to stay with her. She began yelling, "Give me my purse. I've got money!" She was desperate and afraid of dying alone. It was so sad to see her like that. Secret almost burst out crying because she had never seen Picket that way. Due to sobbing uncontrollably, the nurse was called in to give Picket some oxygen and calming medication. As a nurse herself, Secret wanted to reach out and hug the hysterical woman, but she seemed frozen. She grabbed her purse and suddenly ran out of the room. Just then, she began pacing in the hallway. With both hands on top of her head, she said, "Lord, we've got to talk and I mean right now!" She couldn't find the chapel, but she found a restroom. Bending down on her knees she prayed, *Father, I have never prayed in a restroom before, but this is an emergency. You know what I want to do about Picket Jones, but at this point, I need your courage to do the right thing. I really don't even know why I'm talking to you about this because I already know what you want me to do. But doing is the hard part. I'm just asking that you lead me every step of the way because this is a very difficult situation. Amen.*

Secret stopped by the open coffee machine. *Lord, I need a strong cup of coffee with extra cream today. Picket is a mess.* Just then, she heard a still small voice say, "I fixed your life when it was a mess. I can fix anyone and anything." Tears began to run into her hot coffee. Blowing her nose, she smiled knowing that her heavenly Father would give her all the strength she needed. Besides that, it was only last year that she was a real mess also. God had fixed her life when she was a hot mess herself.

She couldn't explain it, but she felt the warm comfort of God while she slowly sipped her coffee. Although she stood in front of Picket's hospital door for a few minutes, it seemed like an eternity. "Come on, Secret, let's do this," she said, motivating herself to go back in.

"Ms. Latisha, how long does she have?" asked Secret as she sat beside Picket on her bed.

"To be honest, we can't say for sure, but it looks as if she has less than six months."

Taking a deep breath, Secret gave Picket a side hug. "I cannot believe I'm doing this, and I know this sounds crazy coming from me, but you need to come home with me."

"No, I couldn't," said Picket, not believing what she just heard.

"Oh, Miss Thing, I think you thought I was giving you an option. I wasn't. You are coming home with me." Picket began to weep again.

"Stop crying before you get dehydrated," said Secret, wiping Picket's tears. "I'll talk to my mother about it, and we'll come up with something, don't worry. Latisha, you can put a check by family support."

"Ms. Bell, I have already heard that you are a good nurse practitioner, so I couldn't have come up with a better plan myself," said Latisha, nearly crying herself.

Secret got as close to Picket's face as she could and whispered, "So I guess I'm going to be your nurse after all. You're going to see this face every day until you die." Secret grinned as she pointed at her face.

Picket let out a tearful laugh. "Oh, Lord, take me now!"

Picket was literally stunned that the lady she had fought several times was taking her to her own house. Secret knew that her life was about to get a lot more complicated, but she had help from heaven and her family. "You lay back and you get you some rest. I'm leaving now."

Picket asked Secret to wait for a minute. "I want to tell you something. I know that I've been very ugly to you. I am truly sorry. I knew that if I took Mercy, that would hurt you and Royce." Secret wanted to pull away, but this time the Christ in her didn't drain out. The Christ in her made her strong enough to embrace a sick and helpless woman.

Picket continued, "That was the only way that I felt that I could spend the last few months with my daughter." Finally releasing Secret's hand, Picket said, "I know you're wondering where Mercy has been. I want to assure you that she has a wonderful nanny who's been taking care of her. But Mercy has never been happy since I brought her home, and she cries for you every night.

Secret thought that she would get joy out of that statement but instead felt saddened that Mercy had suffered so much. "I know that I gave birth to her, but the truth is, you've been more of a mother to her than I've ever been. You rescued her when I abandoned her."

Could Secret be hearing right? Picket was letting it all out, and she seemed to be freeing herself. "I'm sorry for what I've done, but I'm so glad that you were there last year."

"Hey now, you don't have to say all those things."

"No, it's truth, and I've wanted to bring her back so many times, but my pride would not let me. Now, my body is letting me know that I won't be there to raise my own daughter." Picket began to wail.

"Come on now, we have plenty of time for tears. Save some for later."

"Also, I want you to know that there's nothing in me that wants big-headed Royce Storm. When I told you that I was coming back to get him, I only said that because I knew that it would drive you crazy. What we had was in the past, and we have forgiven each other and moved on."

"Don't be talking about my man's big head," Secret said jokingly.

Picket rebuffed, "See, I had obese Royce, but you got the fine Royce. Now, the man is fine, isn't he?"

"And you know this." said Secret, snapping her fingers.

Picket told Secret that she would call the nanny to bring Mercy to Dallas after she was released from the hospital in a few weeks. Secret turned her head and said, "Thank you so much." She quietly closed the door behind her then slid down the wall in the hallway. It had been a long and emotional day at the hospital. Although Secret was initially sent there by Royce's therapist, in reflection she felt that she was actually sent there by a higher power.

Chapter 16

Hattie Goes Home

Helen went through Secret's room to pick up more dirty laundry. Her daughter had been so busy with visiting Royce at rehab, driving to Tyler to check the mail, taking care of justice, and now she was getting the guest room ready for Picket.

A letter fell off the drawer. "What is this?" Helen looked closely and saw that the letter was from Sergeant Davis Patton. Although Helen knew that she should not be reading other people's mail, she could not help it. The letter addressed to Royce was unopened. *Secret must have overlooked it among the other letters*, thought Helen while looking around.

> Dear Royce, I don't know what is going on. I sure hope you're okay. Man, I got something to tell you, but I have to tell you in person. I'm still reading the stack of letters from my biological mother. There is a few more left to read, but I did find out that I am not an only child. I'll be there in two more weeks and hopefully will have some more news about my family. I'm finally sending you a picture of me in uniform! Although I've never seen you, I feel like I've known you all my life.

Helen placed her hand over her mouth. "Lord have mercy," she said in a whisper. Quickly, she tucked the letter and placed it in her pocket and immediately called Shelia. "Girl, I got something to tell you."

"What is it?" asked Shelia.

"You know that project that Hattie has us working on? Well, it just got a little more complicated." She pulled out a picture of Davis Patton just to make sure she was seeing correctly. "Shelia, I think Royce's pen pal is his brother. They look just alike."

Helen grinned and tried to whisper over the phone. "I thought I told you about Royce's military pen pal. Royce's father had been writing this soldier who had no family. But after Royce's father died, they became friends and continued writing each other."

"How nice," said Shelia.

"He will be here in two weeks for the wedding, but he doesn't know that they cancelled it. I am going to write him tonight and tell him what is going on," Helen said.

The family was excited to get together for the Fourth of July because they had all been so busy. Secret, Helen, and Shelia gathered together in the living room of Hattie's house. "How are we going to get Hattie to Arkansas? That's literally the last thing on her list," asked Helen to Secret. Secret told them that she already had that taken care of. They were going to take Hattie by ambulance.

"Really, can we do that?" asked Shelia. Secret told her that Hattie would be sedated on the ride there. It would take hours to get there, but she would be comfortable. Hattie's morphine pump would be constantly monitored to make sure she was without pain.

Secret whispered, "To tell you the truth, the doctor was against it at first, but he told me that he would do the same thing for his mother. He checked my nurse practitioner certificate to make sure that it was up to date. He only agreed to let me take her if I got a hospice nurse to accompany us to Arkansas. Her name is Jackie Jackson, and she is very nice." Helen and Shelia thought that was definitely a great idea since there were so many things going on. "The Last Wish Foundation is paying for the gas and the nurse's salary."

The table was set with barbecue chicken, potato salad, baked beans, macaroni, and chocolate cake. Everyone laughed as Justice put both of his hands in the cake and ate it. In all the laughs and fireworks, Secret noticed that Hattie ate little even though the menu was full of her favorite foods.

"How is Granny doing, Shelia?" asked Secret outside of Hattie's room.

"Well, she turns her head and refuses to eat most days. She told me that she is ready to go home. Hattie seems more disconnected each day."

All of Hattie's sisters whispered to each other while they sat on the couch. "We don't even have a place to stay down there. That farm is probably not even there anymore. We all left over fifty years ago," said MaryAnn.

"We'll probably stay at a hotel close to the old farm and go visit," said Mae.

Jean said, "I know y'all don't understand, but I just can't go back there! I just can't." She cried.

Mae grabbed Jean and said, "Sis, if I can go back, I know you can. We both know what happened there, don't we, Jean?" Mae looked at Jean side-eyed as if she knew a secret. Jean got up and walked out crying. The other sisters wondered what all the crying was about, but no one asked.

Secret gently rubbed her grandmother's hand, waking her up. "Granny, we are taking you back home next week. Will you hold on for me?"

"Yes, baby. I am going home, and I am so happy. It's been so long," said Hattie.

Hattie's sisters weren't as excited to go back to the place of so much past pain, but they agreed. Actually they all had painful memories on the farm in Arkansas, but they also had some good ones. "If Hattie wants to go back home, then we'll go back home," said Lee to her sisters.

The rest of the day was mostly peaceful, and everyone hugged before they went to their own homes. Helen and Shelia stayed with Hattie due to both of them fearing that she had very little time left.

Secret's phone beeped early the next morning. She was all smiles as Picket texted her that she was being released in a few hours. She had to remind herself why she was taking in her enemy, but she was also a Christian and knew what she had to do. Besides, Secret felt sorry for Picket, and although she didn't have as much money as Picket, she did have a good family.

"You look better, Miss Thing," said Secret to her new housemate.

Picket smacked her lips and said, "You know what, I feel a lot better. At least I have more time with Mercy." Picket noticed that Secret seemed somewhat distant and her lips turned downward.

"Hey now, I don't need to you crying about that. I thought we had that settled. Both of us will take care of her," said Picket.

Secret wiped her teary eyes and told her that she was thinking about her grandmother not being a part of her life anymore. Picket didn't know anything that was going on with Secret's family, but Secret told her the entire story. "We are taking Granny back to Arkansas as her final wish."

"I didn't know that you were going through such a hard time.

"So when are y'all leaving to take your grandmother to Arkansas?" asked Picket.

Secret told her that it would need to be very soon. "I hate to admit it, but Granny could go at any day."

Picket looked down, thinking that technically she could go at any day too. Picket asked if she and Mercy would need to stay at her house while they went to Arkansas. "Uh, no, I don't trust you alone at my house. I guess you and Mercy are going with us to Arkansas."

"Are you sure?"

"Yes, the way I see it, you are basically family, and we are here to help you too."

Picket loved her new room due to all the flowers that Secret had placed in there. Later that evening, Mercy arrived full of smiles. She was somewhat confused but hugged both of her mothers. Picket wasn't even upset when Mercy slept in her old toddler bed in Secret's room. Picket laughed as Justice and Mercy wrestled each other on the floor. They played together all night long. "I think I'm going to be happy here," said Picket. She didn't find it the least bit awkward that she was living with her ex-enemy.

Secret went to check on Royce over the next few days and was so happy to see him doing better. He had even begun preparing recipes with the kitchen staff as part of his rehab. They allowed him to stir, season, and even cook a few small dishes. Each day he looked forward to being released. His love for his bride-to-be grew deeper and deeper as she continued to be his cheerleader. Late each evening, he'd call her as she cried about her grandmother's pending death. Indeed, Secret was under a lot of stress, but she relied on her faith to keep her strong.

Secret came for her daily visit and noticed that Royce had a big smile on his face. "What are you so happy about? Are you ready to be discharged?" she asked.

"No, that's not it. I did get some good news, though. I'll tell you about it later."

"Great, we could all use some good news about now. Babe, I think it's time that we take Granny to Arkansas. She's fading, and this is her very last wish."

Royce had been there when Granny Bell asked Secret to help her fulfill her last few wishes. He smiled and kissed Secret's hand softly and said, "This must be so hard for you. I can't even imagine what you must be going through." Royce and Secret slowly walked over to a couch in the lobby. He continued, "Secret, I don't have any family left, but your family has embraced me like one of their own. I felt so alone before I met you and your family." Royce pulled out the blue envelope that Hattie had given him months ago. He told Secret that he held it close to his heart, and he planned to always keep it as a token from Hattie. Royce had grown to love Granny Bell as if she were his own grandmother.

"We didn't even get to find out who was the best cook in the family," said Royce, rubbing his hands together. "It would be old school against new school."

"Oh, honey, we didn't need a contest for that because my granny would have beat you like you stole something." They held hands, and both laughed as Royce rolled his eyes at Secret.

"I have to go, but you keep up the good work. I expect to see you standing tall when I get back." Secret gave her fiancé a kiss and a hug. Upon leaving the rehab, she saw Shelia's van. *Maybe she has another client here*, she thought.

Hattie had a rough night, and Helen called the doctor early the next morning. He usually didn't make house calls, but he had known Hattie for at least thirty years. This was her last doctor's appointment because he told them she would be gone within a week or so. Her breathing had become somewhat labored, and she had nearly stopped eating. She still gave a smile every now and then, but it was clear she was waiting on her "chariot to come." After he examined her, he told them that her organs were beginning to slowly shut down.

"Secret, it's time to get your grandmother to Arkansas," said Helen during their phone call. Helen's job was to get everyone else together for the trip. Shelia drove everyone in her van. "I want my baby to ride back here with me," whispered Hattie to Shelia. Secret's plan was for Hattie to be sedated during the long ride to Arkansas. However, Hattie objected and asked to remain fully awake during the ride. With a twinkle in her eye, Hattie said, "I don't want to miss a thing."

"Granny, guess what? I wrote a song for you."

Although Hattie had nearly been unresponsive to most people, she smiled and squeezed her granddaughter's hand. With her eyes closed, she said, "Go on and sing for Granny, baby."

She hadn't sung since she was molested at age twelve. Her voice had been silenced by a terrible evil, but somehow she felt free now. She had only grown stronger in her mind, body, and soul over the years.

"Don't be nervous," whispered Hattie.

The ambulance drivers gave a quick glance at the patient in the back but smiled as Secret began to sing.

"If stilettoes could walk, if stilettoes could talk they would be talking about the golden streets. If stilettoes could move, if stilettoes could groove, they would be dancing on the golden streets."

Secret grinned as Granny Bell wiggled her feet to the beat. The hospice nurse, Jackie, smiled and held Hattie's hand as she moved her feet to the rhythm at Secret's beautiful soprano voice. Secret sang it over and over because Granny kept asking her to sing the stiletto song.

It took some hours to get to Conway, Arkansas; but besides the few restroom breaks, everyone arrived in good spirits. Everyone except Shelia and Hattie was in for a huge surprise. Everyone noticed a work crew putting up a large sign over the long gravel road leading to the property. Due to the sign being turned around, no one could read it.

"Wait a minute, this is not the same place, is it, Lee?" asked Jean, looking around. "This GPS has to be wrong. Our farm should have been run down a long time ago." There were no run-down houses, barns, or tractors anywhere on the property. There rested a gorgeous large log cabin surrounded by all types of tulips, roses, and sunflowers. The rich, luscious green grass looked more like plush carpet than real grass. To the east of the cabin was a beautiful glistening pond with a family of white swans and lily pads all over it. Most of the large shade trees had hammocks and swings attached to them.

"What is that sweet smell?" asked Mae. To her left and right were several rose gardens. It seemed that the gardens were full of red, white, peach, yellow, and blue roses. The sweet smell covered the entire property.

MaryAnn said, "I think our farm is actually down the road."

Shelia asked everyone to get off the van, but Hattie's sisters seemed afraid to get off. Shelia assured them that this was the correct address. Had the farm been sold?

"Aunt Jean, you told me that the old farm was tacky and run-down. But this place is immaculate!" exclaimed Secret.

Picket grabbed Mercy by the hand and said, "We ain't standing around looking. Let's go, girl. Come on, Justice, let's go see some swans."

Justice squealed, "Yes, birds," while pointing at several beautiful white swimming swans.

"I know you are all shocked, but your sister had fixed it up many years ago," said Shelia, leading them to the cabin.

"How do you know, Shelia?" asked Mae.

"Because Hattie told me about this and several other things. Ladies, your sister also has a few other surprises for you."

Just then, a smiling man came out of the cabin while extending his hand to Helen. "Hello, it's so good to finally meet you all. My name is Reverend Billy White, but most folks just call me Rev." Everyone still looked confused, except Shelia. "I can tell by the looks on your faces that you all are surprised to see me. I've been taking care of this property for several years now. Doesn't it look great? We've even had large rose-covered gates added onto the entrance of the garden."

"How could Hattie not tell us about this?" whispered MaryAnn to Jean.

"Well, I guess she had a reason. Let's go inside." Shelia gave the signal for the ambulance drivers to open the back doors and bring their patient out. Although Hattie was somewhat sleepy, she gave a faint smirk as she was rolled past her sisters.

Lee hollered out, "Hattie, we need to talk about this!"

Jackie walked beside the gurney. The crackling, roaring fireplace was going inside of the air-conditioned cabin. Thick plush white rugs were artfully arranged all over the floor. There were blue and white gardenias in glass lighted vases on every end table. Helen looked up and saw sparkling chandeliers that hung in every room of the house. Elegance and the beauty of the cabin could not be denied.

"Wow," said Picket as she looked around. "I come from money, and even I've never seen anything so beautiful."

Reverend White showed everyone to their rooms. The log cabin had seven beautiful fully furnished bedrooms, and each room had a different theme.

Jean said, "Reverend White, why is it that we were surprised to see you, but you are not surprised to see us?"

He smiled and said, "Hattie has been coming down here for many years. She's the one who picked out the decorations, the different themes of the rooms, and even the swans in the pond. Your sister helped plant every single rosebush and garden. Follow me. I want to show you something." Reverend White showed the ladies Hattie's vegetable and herb garden. She had all kinds of herbs and spices used for cooking. The smell of basil, oregano, and parsley filled the air. A lady waved at them as she picked spices and vegetables from the garden. Helen picked a large peach hanging from a nearby peach tree. "She told me that she'd come back here one day, but she had to wait until the right time," he said, eating a plum off the plum tree.

"Reverend White, where did Hattie get all the money from to fix up this place?" asked Lee.

"I don't know," he said.

Shelia interrupted, "I'm trying to tell y'all, Hattie is not broke."

Hattie's room had already been set up with all kinds of medical supplies that she would need.

"Granny, you thought of everything, didn't you?" Secret said, patting her hand.

Hattie gave a quaint smile and said, "Yes."

"Is everyone hungry?" asked a full-figured Caucasian lady walking from the kitchen.

"Who are you?" asked Mae.

"Ladies, I'm your chef for the time you'll be here. I'm Gina, and I can cook anything you want," she said, smiling. "Most of my recipes are right from Hattie's own garden." Jean looked at Gina and rolled her eyes and folded her arms. "I bet I know what you are thinking," said Gina. "You are thinking that this white lady can't cook soul food."

"Well, you said it," said Jean.

Gina said, "Well, in the South, we all eat Southern food, soul food, and just good old country eating."

Mae and Lee both gave Gina a high five and said, "Girl, you are telling the truth," said Lee. I know some white ladies who can tear it up in the kitchen." They all laughed.

Mae whispered, "Jean, you should be ashamed of yourself. Hattie wouldn't have chosen her if she couldn't cook." After a delicious dinner, Jean apologized due to Gina cooking some of the best soul food they had ever tasted.

Chapter 17

The Broken Mirror

Davis Patton was beyond excited as his plane landed at the Dallas Airport. He rented a car and drove to the David Conner Rehab Center. He couldn't wait to tell Royce that he had discovered they were probably brothers. Davis had their biological father's military flag and their mother's letters in hand.

Helen had written him and made him aware of all the happenings of the last few months. He had no idea that his pen pal had not been getting his letters nor had he been in any position to respond. As a military man, he was not usually nervous meeting unfamiliar persons, but Royce was not just any stranger. After all the years of writing each other, Davis never knew that he was writing his own sibling.

Entering the rehab, the new civilian struggled to get his nerves under control. *What if Royce is not actually my brother? What if all of this is some kind of mistake? What if Royce rejects me?* Davis nearly turned around and walked back out the door upon entering the rehab. He had so many questions, doubts, and now fears of rejection. Due to struggling to collect his thoughts, the former marine decided to sit in the lobby for a few minutes. "Hey, you finally got discharged. All that hard work paid off," said one of his therapists, giving Davis a thumbs-up.

"What?" Davis was bewildered due to a stranger talking to him.

"Man, that food was delicious. I heard you were the one calling the shots in the kitchen today," said another patient rolling by in a wheelchair. He returned the thumbs to him also. He figured he'd go find Royce before any other strangers spoke to him.

"Excuse me, do you know what room Royce Storm is in?" asked Davis at the nurses' station.

"Mr. Storm, please stop playing and get back to your room. You've been walking one day without your walker, and now you're trying to show out. Where's your cane? You're not discharged yet. One more day, sir." The nurse took Davis by the hand and walked him out unknowingly to Royce's room. "All right now, here you go," she said, opening the door. To her surprise, Royce was lying in bed watching TV. She looked at Royce and the stranger and apologized to them both.

Royce abruptly sat up and asked, "What is going on here?"

"Man, it's me, Davis . . . Davis Patton." Like a young deer in headlights, he seemed frozen in his tracks. For a moment, he stood in one place shaking his head and rubbing his eyes. "My god, man, I don't believe it," said Davis.

"You don't believe it! Man, I don't believe what I'm seeing either," said Royce as his mouth hung open.

"Royce, I just found out that there was a possibility that we could be brothers a few days ago. I wondered if it could be true or was everything that I found out a coincidence. But, bruh, I ain't got to wonder no more. Dude, you have my face, my eyes, and my body!"

The two men looked identical in every way. Royce knew that he was coming for the wedding, but he had forgotten all about it. Royce still couldn't speak due to him being still in disbelief. He just gazed at his identical twin who was standing there talking to him.

Snapping out of his shock, Royce said, "Brother, Davis, man . . . I'm so confused right now, I don't know what to call you."

"Royce, we are brothers," said Davis.

"Uh, yes, I can see that. Looks like we are more than that." They were obviously identical twins, but how could they not know?

Several months prior, Davis had written a letter to his stepfather asking him for more information about his adoption. Although his late wife rarely discussed it, Michael Patton sent Davis as information as he had found among his wife's things.

"I've found a stack of old letters in your mother's shoebox and a military flag in an old suitcase. I am sure you will find some helpful information in here." The package from Mr. Patton arrived only a few weeks before Davis was discharged.

"Is that a flag?" asked Royce, pointing to an object under his brother's arm. Davis pulled out the neatly folded American flag.

"Yes, but this isn't any ordinary flag. This was the flag from our father's funeral. Sergeant James Cook was our father's name. He was a real tough hero in the Marines and died in a helicopter crash just two weeks from getting discharged. A helicopter went down with him and his entire crew still in it," said Davis. "The funny thing is that I was always drawn to the military, and now I know why. I have much respect for that flag."

"Much respect, brother, and thank you for your service. They would have kicked me out of there because I'm a lot of things, but a soldier isn't one of them. Did you find out what happened to our mother?" asked Royce.

"Yes, her name was Carolyn Cook, and she died of cancer a few months before our father died."

Both of them shook their heads and said, "That's a real shame," at the same time.

Davis continued, "Evidently, she started writing us these letters when she found out she had a few months to live. She even wrote on the night that she died. From reading our mom's letters, she left you with her pastor and wife while our dad took her to the hospital."

"Would that happen to be Mary and Leroy Storm?" asked Royce as if he were putting a puzzle together.

"Yep, that's exactly who kept you, but she left me with our dad's cousin, Regina."

"That must be how they got the letters," muttered Royce.

Davis said, "Evidently my adoptive mother saved my letters, but she never gave them to me."

Royce said, "I wonder why I didn't know about any of this. I never got any letters."

"But none of that explains how we got separated. They were supposed to be watching us for a while, not forever." Davis noticed the same wrinkle in Royce's forehead as he had in his.

Davis explained that since both of their parents died so suddenly, they were left in the custody of their father's cousin, Regina Cook.

"Even after reading the letters, I still needed my stepdad's help to put the rest of the pieces together. Not only were we adopted and separated, my name was changed."

The twins didn't realize how much they were bonding with each other. They were talking like old friends and actually felt like they had never been apart.

Davis moved his chair closer to Royce's bed and poured himself a cup of water. "My stepfather told me the entire story as best he could. Evidently, our cousin fell in love with a loser who didn't want any children. Since she had both of us, she decided to leave one of us behind, you."

"Really?"

Davis apologized on behalf of Regina. "She felt that you had bonded with the Storms more than I had. Regina ran off to West Virginia with me.

Royce shook his head in disbelief. "Man, this is quite a story you are telling me."

"It's true, and she was so embarrassed after the man left her that she completely changed my name from William to Davis. She didn't want the Storms to search for me. When she married Mr. Patton, he adopted me, and I took his last name. My real name is William Cook, and your name was Royce Cook before you were adopted." Davis told Royce that he always wondered why Reverend Storm chose him as a pen pal rather than another soldier. "Looking back, I think Reverend Storm knew that I was your brother all along. I told him my mother's name in one of my letters," said Davis.

"I am still a little in shocked that not only do I have a brother, but a twin at that. I thought I was alone all this time," cried Royce.

"Man, don't start all of that. Stop it! I'm a soldier. I can't cry."

"Then why do I see tears in your eyes? I'm the one with the head injury. Are you going to keep looking at me or hug me?"

Davis couldn't resist hugging his brother because he had felt alone his entire life. Both of them started sobbing but quickly tried to get themselves together. "Secret is going to be so surprised," said Royce.

"Speaking of Secret, what is going on with the wedding? A lady named Helen wrote me and told me about your car accident and injury. She told me the wedding had been cancelled, but they were still hopeful things would work out."

Royce told Davis that Secret had cancelled the summer wedding, but Secret's family had planned another surprise for her, in Arkansas. "Davis, how would you feel driving me to Arkansas to surprise my fiancée?"

"Bro, you already know I'm down for whatever. Besides, that will give us time to catch up on everything."

Davis pulled out a custom-made wooden mahogany cane and handed it to Royce.

"As soon as I heard about your injuries, I had this made for you. You are going to be sharp as a tack."

"All right now. This is nice, man."

Royce and Davis had both been surprised by each other. Each felt proud of their father's military service and their mother's courage to write them letters. She hoped they would have a good life, and she tried to live for them. Royce cried as he read each and every letter from his mother. It appeared that her hopes for them had come true after all. In one of her letters, she wrote a prayer that asked God to bring them back together if they were ever separated. God had heard her prayer and did exactly that.

Chapter 18

Secret's Gift

Secret struggled to get out of her grandmother's hospital bed without making a noise. It didn't help that she had to wear her shiny red wedding stilettos in a hospital bed. Hattie insisted that Secret wear her wedding shoes beside her red stilettos.

"No one ever seen two women in high heels laying in a hospital bed together." Secret laughed to Hattie.

"And they won't see it now either." Granny had asked her to sleep with her just like she did when she was a toddler. "Are you trying to sneak out of the bed?" asked Hattie sleepily. "You look like a caterpillar in a cocoon."

"Granny, I'm so sorry. I didn't want to wake you," whispered Secret.

Both laughed when Hattie said, "Baby, I know I asked you to hold me, but that back side done grew up."

"Granny, don't be talking about my back side." Secret reminded her grandmother that she was thirty-three years old. She smiled as Hattie kissed her cheek and said, "You'll always be my baby." Hattie couldn't help but cry thinking of how much she would miss her granddaughter.

"Why are you crying, Granny?"

"I'm just hurting, that's all."

"Is the morphine pump not working anymore? We can turn it up."

"Baby, I don't mean that kind of agony. My heart hurts because I am going to miss you when I leave, but I have to go, sweetie. My time has run out. Secret, can you hold Granny for ten more minutes?"

If she goes while I'm holding her, I am going to lose it, Secret said to herself, trying to hold back her tears.

Secret barely made it out of the bed the first time but managed to get back in and fell asleep holding her grandmother. Hattie pretended to be asleep, but she kissed a sleeping Secret on her tearstained cheek. She gave a faint grin thinking of how she held a then-two-year-old Secret. Now a thirty-something-year-old Secret was holding her. *It's funny how things turn around*, thought Hattie, gazing at how beautiful her granddaughter had become.

Stretching then yawning, Secret had almost forgotten where she was. The last few months had been exhausting physically and emotionally. Secret reached over and took Hattie's pulse due to her sleeping so soundly. "Thank God. Granny, don't scare me like that."

Hattie grinned as she felt Secret's finger on her wrist. "You can't stop being a nurse even for a minute, can you? Don't worry, I'm still alive."

"Granny, what do you want to do today? You wanted to come back home, so here we are."

"I'm getting ready for a wedding."

"What? Whose wedding? Granny, you know my wedding was cancelled until next year. There was just too much going on to plan a wedding."

"Well, baby, all I know is somebody is getting married today."

"Who?" Secret climbed out of the hospital bed and loudly called her mother who was down the hall. "Mom!" No one answered Secret's desperate holler down the hallway. "Helen Ruffins! Mom!"

Just then, Helen swung open her room door. "I was in the shower, and you know better than calling me Helen. What is it, girl?"

"Mom, Granny is talking crazy in here. She said something about a wedding today. Do you know what she's talking about?"

"Oh, girl, I thought something had really happened in here. Aunt Lee, Aunt Mae, Aunt Jean, Aunt MaryAnn . . . y'all come here."

They all came into Hattie's room and asked what was going on. "Mom told Secret that there's gonna be a wedding today." They all smiled and shrugged their shoulders. Secret frowned and placed both hands on her hips. They all turned around and walked out of the room.

"No, y'all didn't! What are you not telling me?" asked Secret while following them to the kitchen. She stopped in her tracks as Gina pointed to a chair that had a sign on it. "I think this is your chair that says 'bride-to-be,'" she said, smiling. "Do you see anything you like?"

"Uh, yes." She looked around at the breakfast buffet surrounding her. It was hard for her to choose due to Gina preparing fluffy blueberry muffins, buttermilk strawberry waffles, cheesy omelets with three different types of sausage, fluffy buttermilk biscuits, and several different types of flavored coffee.

"Gina, I don't know what kind of training you had; but, girl, this looks delicious."

Gina smiled and said, "Thank you, but I was actually trained by your grandmother. You know, Ms. Bell, you are going to make a beautiful bride." She poured her a hot delicious cup of vanilla coffee.

"Thank you, but my wedding is not until next year."

"Really? That's funny because the wedding caterers are already setting up the tables outside in the rose garden."

"What!" Secret ran out of the kitchen in her pajamas and saw dozens of tables being decorated with all types of red roses and white lilies. She saw her ex-enemy sitting there building her a flower-colored wedding arch.

"Picket, what are you doing?"

"Nothing." Picket smiled while she continued to build. "So I see that you know about your surprise by now."

"What do they got you out here doing?"

"Lord have mercy, I see you got on the supershoes. Are you going to fight me again?" Picket jokingly held her hands up in a defensive mode.

Secret swatted at her and said, "Girl, stop playing."

Secret felt so confused, but the arch was simply breathtaking. It had been painted glistening silver with red roses intertwined with white strings of large pearls and emerald-green ivy plants. A string of elegant white lights we're intertwined with every rose.

"Picket, can you tell me what is going on here?"

"I know you didn't know, but my major in college was architecture. Your grandmother and her glam squad had everything for the wedding, except an arch where you are supposed to stand. So I volunteered to build you one." Picket looked down and continued to work, then she smiled and pointed behind Secret. Turning around, she saw Mae, Lee, MaryAnn, Jean, Helen, and Shelia holding a sign saying, "Surprise, you are getting married today."

Secret began to shout, "What are y'all talking about? I don't have a dress, a groom, bridesmaids, or a reverend!"

"All that is taken care of," said Helen, hugging her bewildered daughter. "Reverend White is already here, remember." Why did the bride-to-be still feel so clueless? Helen gently placed both hands on her daughter's shoulders. "Secret, if it wasn't for you, your grandmother wouldn't have lived as long and happy as she has. By bringing her home to Arkansas, you granted her last wish. But in return, this wedding was her last gift to you. She has planned the wedding of your dreams. I know you rescheduled your wedding until next year, but looks like to me, there will be a wedding this summer. In fact, there will be a wedding today."

The bride-to-be collapsed to her knees with grateful tears. "Oh, Granny, how could you? And none of you old birds told me about this. Usually, y'all can't hold water." She turned and pointed at Picket, "And you, Miss Thing . . ."

Picket held up her hands in her defense and responded, "Hey, don't blame me. I just found out about this last night."

"Now, are you gonna finish your delicious breakfast? Looks like you have a big day ahead," said Gina.

"Hurry up, we're going to get your hair done as soon as you get your clothes on," said Helen, pushing her daughter back to the cabin. "There is a lady in town who is the best of the best at bridal hairstyles. Baby, you are going to look so beautiful." There was also a makeup artist there to make her even more beautiful than she already was.

"Mom, what about my dress? I still don't have a dress here in Arkansas. Is there a bridal shop nearby?"

Helen and her aunts all laughed. "Your dress is already here. Secret, do you remember the dress that you saw at the mall a few months ago?"

"Sure, remember I picked it out and got fitted for it. I sure hated to cancel everything, but I had to send the dress back." Secret shook her head thinking of how beautiful the dress was.

"Baby girl, I'm not talking about the one that you sent back. I'm talking about the dress of your dreams."

Secret placed both hands over her mouth due to complete shock. "Mom, do you mean the off-the-shoulder ivory ball gown with the lace V-neck? It can't be the one with the cathedral lace train?"

"Girl, you have a great memory and detailed too. Yes, Secret, that's the one I'm talking about."

"That dress was thousands of dollars! I couldn't even try it on because it was too expensive and too huge to fit inside the fitting room stall. That dress?"

"Yep, that's the one." Helen's face seemed to be oozing with excitement. "That's the one your grandmother sent me back to get. We already had your measurements, so it was no problem. Your grandmother just wanted to know what the dress of your dreams was."

"My goodness. I can't believe this!" Secret started to collapse again and couldn't help but to sob. She was overwhelmed with joy and hysteria.

"Look here, you are going to get dehydrated if you don't stop it," said Picket mockingly. The bride-to-be was nervous, excited, and grateful; and she could not seem to get herself together.

All of her aunts said, "Come on, baby, sit here and finish your breakfast." They gathered around her and began to spoon-feed her like they all did when she was a toddler.

"All right, all right now!" said Secret while shooing them away. Looking at Helen, Secret said, "Mom, none of my bridesmaids are here? I didn't get to tell any of friends about this, because I didn't know about it myself."

Aunt MaryAnn kissed her great-niece on the cheek and said, "Oh, honey, you got bridesmaids. We all may be just a little older, but we will bring the heat!" she said, snapping her fingers.

Mae and Lee all shook their heads and smiled. "We are going to look fabulous," they said.

"I have truly never seen bridesmaids as old as y'all. It's going to take y'all forever to get down the aisle," said Secret with a chuckle.

"You better stop it before we all get in line to spank those bridal hips," MaryAnn said, swatting at her great-niece.

Helen said, "I bet you've never seen a fifty-two-year-old flower girl either."

"Oh no, Mom, you wouldn't!"

"Yes, I am. I'm going to be a flower woman!"

What kind of a wedding will this be? she thought as she smiled and sipped her coffee. They all laughed and looked around for Jean, but she had gone back to her cabin room.

Chapter 19

The Old Bones Say Goodbye

All the ladies, except Jean, seemed excited to be getting their hair done. Secret and the rest of the ladies went to get dressed for the exciting day ahead.

"Come on, Jean, let's go. You been dragging all morning. Are you okay, sis?" asked MaryAnn, beckoning her sister to get inside Shelia's van. Jean told everyone that she left her medicine inside the cabin.

Looking around to see if anyone else was in Hattie's room, Jean quietly eased beside her bed.

Jackie creaked open the door and saw Jean standing there. "I'm so sorry, but she's not going to last much longer. I just hope she can last through Secret's wedding," said Jackie. "I'll give you two some time alone. I'll just take a coffee break because I know this is going to be a long day."

Jean leaned over and grabbed her sister's hand. She began to weep as she whispered something into her ear. Hattie opened her eyes and glared at Jean.

"Hattie, I'm sorry. I should have told you sooner, but I just didn't know how you react. Please forgive me. I've held this for so long, but I'm going to make it right today. I promise."

Hattie took shallow breaths as she spoke, but she whispered, "No, Jean, it's okay now."

Just then, Jackie came into the room to check her patient's blood pressure. "Is everything okay, Ms. Jean?" There was no answer due to Jean quickly exiting the room.

Secret, Helen, and her aunts giggled with excitement like wide-eyed teenage girls going to the prom. Jean seemed distant, but she tried to put on a smile for her niece's big day. Everyone was focused on the bridal shop, but Jean noticed the Conway Police Department next door to the boutique. As they walked into the building, a lady with open arms walked over to them. "Hello, ladies, we've been expecting you. My name is Thomasia, and this is my team of people that will be working with you today. I must say y'all are a beautiful group of ladies, and I'm not just saying that."

Secret whispered, "Mom, she has an entire team."

Thomasia pulled Secret out of the group and said, "Darling, you've got to be the bride-to-be."

"Yes, ma'am."

"Girl, you look like a woman in love! I have a special room just for you." Secret grinned as she was escorted to a separate dressing room. "My goodness, I have got the perfect style for you and all of this beautiful long hair. You are going to truly be the brown bombshell today." Secret couldn't remember the last time that she felt so pampered. Between her first husband being murdered two years prior, her grandmother's illness, and then all the drama with her new love this year, there was little time for pampering. "Sister girl, you are simply gorgeous. It's not going to take me long to just bring out your natural beauty."

Looking at her team of makeup artists and hairstylists, Thomasia said, "All right, dream team, let's get started." Like soldiers, they grabbed their hair curlers, pearls, beaded combs, brushes, blow-dryers, and all colors of makeup.

These elderly women had a natural elegance even with their silver hair. Jean rushed her personal team due to needing to run a quick errand downtown. MaryAnn said, "Jean, you haven't been to downtown Conway in over fifty years. What business do you have over here?" Jean told everyone that she would find a ride back to the cabin. She just wanted to get a gift for Hattie.

"You know what, Jean, I know you're hiding something," whispered Mae.

Davis and Royce both became hungry because they had been traveling for a few hours. They talked as all the women tried not to stare at them eating together. A few women giggled because they thought they recognized Royce from his cookbook. The brothers ate and talked over steak and eggs. "What would you like to do now that you're out here with all of us civilians?" asked Royce.

"I figured that since I love building things, I may as well open my own construction company. I've been thinking about that for over a year now."

Just then, a group of excited women walked over to the table and handed Davis several napkins. "Excuse me, sir, would you please sign our napkins?" they all asked. Davis asked why they wanted him to sign their napkins. Just then, Royce grabbed the napkins and said, "Give me these. I'd love to sign them, ladies." They all smiled and even gave him several of their phone numbers.

"Oh, I'm sorry, ladies. I'm getting married later today," said Royce to one beautiful young lady.

Davis interjected, raising one finger, "But I'm not! I'll take your number, sweetie." All the women giggled and walked back to their table.

"Man, did you forget to tell me something?" asked Davis with his shoulders raised.

Being the shy man that he was, Royce held his head down and said, "I wrote a cookbook that mainly women seem to love. Secret said that the recipes were good, but my picture on the back was better. Can you believe that Secret called me eye candy for the ladies?"

Davis let out a loud laugh. "So I guess I'd be eye candy too, Chocolate Thunder."

"Stop, man, my ribs hurt when I laugh too hard. I'm still healing."

Royce called Helen and told her that he would be there in a few hours.

"Okay, and you should have seen your bride when she found out about the surprise wedding. She can't wait to see you."

Royce smiled imagining her face and tears. She had been through so much hardship lately.

Jean put on her dark shades, looked around, and walked into the Conway Police Department. "Son, I need to talk to an officer."

"Ma'am, do you want to file a police report?" asked the desk clerk without even looking up at her.

"Stop asking me questions! I need to talk to an officer now. It's important." Jean's hands began to tremble as she started crying uncontrollably.

"All right, ma'am, sit right here," said a young officer who walked from behind the desk. He turned around and whispered into his radio, "Detective Allen, there's an old lady up here demanding to talk to someone. She said it's really important."

"It's all right, ma'am, you can talk to me," said Detective Allen, patting her on the shoulder.

With tear-filled eyes, Jean looked up at him and asked, "Can we talk privately? I have information about a murder that took place here in Conway."

"What? How do you know about the murder? Whose murder? When?" he asked in disbelief. "Did you witness a crime?"

"No, I'm the one who committed a crime," sobbed Jean. "I killed someone!" Jean sobbed into her handkerchief as the detective looked around to see if anyone else had heard what she said. He couldn't believe that an old lady was sitting in his office confessing to a murder.

"Excuse me please," said Detective Allen, walking out quickly. "Lieutenant King, Sergeant Tilley, come with me please." The confused detective didn't hesitate to get assistance with this case. Was the old lady crazy, or did she really kill someone? All three officers walked in Detective Allen's office and took seats beside Jean. "Now, madam, tell them what you told me."

Jean began telling all of the officers that fifty years ago, she killed a man named James Ruffins.

"He was a horrible man who was married to my sister Hattie Bell. After he married Hattie, he then tried to do God knows what with my sister Mae, but I caught him in the act. He threatened to kill me and my other sisters if I told anyone." The detective didn't know if he needed a lie detector test or not. He took notes as she recounted the story.

"One day, in another fit of rage, he shoved Hattie off the porch. She was eight months pregnant, and his push is what killed the baby. My sister lay there bleeding in pain for hours. Instead of helping her, he grabbed a bottle of liquor and a shovel from the barn. By the time my sisters and I got home, he was nowhere around."

"Did anyone else witness this?" asked Detective Allen. Jean told him that the only other witness was Hattie, but she was gravely ill. Jean began to weep thinking of her dying sister and all that she had suffered. "Then what happened?" he asked.

"Well, I never told my sisters, but I sped off in Hattie's car and looked all over town for him. I didn't know what I'd do if I found him. Just when I had nearly stopped looking, I saw him digging a grave at the edge of our property. I asked him what he was doing, and he said, 'I'm going to put Hattie and that dead baby right here.' He knew he had killed the baby, but he didn't care."

Sergeant Tilley handed Jean another tissue as she talked awhile then cried awhile. They all just looked at each other wondering what they would do after her confession.

"I told him I would never allow him to hurt my sister again. He was drunker than he'd ever been and was almost out of his mind. All I saw was hate in his eyes, and it scared me. James lunged at me with the shovel raised over his head. I fell backward and nearly fell into the grave he had just dug. He tried to hit me with the shovel, but I rolled out of the way. However, I was so scared that I kicked him where the sun don't shine. Then I snatched the shovel and swung as hard as I could. James grabbed his head and fell backward into the very grave that he dug. I didn't know that I killed him! I just wanted to stop him from hurting my family." Jean wept and clutched Detective Allen's hand. "Do you believe me, son?"

He told her that he didn't know if he believed her, but he was willing to hear more. Finally without any more prodding, Jean said, "After I realized that he was dead, I threw all the dirt on top of him. I lied and told my sisters that he left."

It was obvious that Jean had kept this secret for decades, and coming back to the farm had brought up her painful past.

"If you got away with it, then why are you confessing to us now? We weren't even alive back then," said Lieutenant King. Jean told them that due to her sister dying, she had come back to the same property where the body was buried. They all excused themselves to discuss what in the world to do with all this information. They possibly had a body and a fifty-year-old crime.

"Ma'am, would you be willing to show us where the body is?" asked Detective Allen.

"Yes, then you can arrest me and take me to jail. I can't live like this anymore," she said, weeping.

Helen received a text from Shelia stating that Hattie was failing fast, but she didn't want Secret to know. Hattie wanted Secret to focus on her big day and not her death. Helen quietly showed the text to all of Hattie's sisters, and they all agreed not to tell Secret. Everyone was happy and sad at the same time. Secret had been separated from the other ladies while she was getting all the special attention that a bride deserves. The blushing bride had not seen herself, but she was anxious to see her hair and makeup. Thomasia asked Lee, MaryAnn, Mae, and Helen to gather in front of the door. "Introducing the brown bombshell, the soon-to-be Mrs. Secret Storm, and the most beautiful woman in Conway, Arkansas, Ms. Secret Bell!" Two of the dream team members placed a large body-length mirror directly in front of the door. Opening the door, Secret gasped and placed both of her hands over her mouth. She couldn't believe how beautiful she looked with her hair in long loose streaked curls. The glam squad placed a large diamond rhinestone-covered crown on her head. The long thin laced ivory wedding veil hung on to the back of the crown. Secret began to cry through her fake eyelashes.

"Oh no! There will be no crying today. I worked too hard on that pretty face for you to cry all my work off." Thomasia took a damp cloth and dabbed Secret's makeup. "Don't worry, my team and I will all be at the wedding to make sure you all look beautiful today."

All the ladies gathered around Secret, and each gave her a hug. Secret looked at her elderly great-aunts and had never seen them so beautiful. They had been plucked, threaded, and tweezed to no end. "Girl, that was the first and last time I'm getting my eyebrows threaded. I almost came out of that chair," said Mae to Lee.

"I'm going to call y'all the silver cougar squad," said Thomasia laughing. Each woman had a chance to see themselves in a full-length mirror. Indeed, their beauty surpassed all age limits, and they didn't know whether to laugh or to cry.

"All right, ladies, let's go. We have to get back and rest before we get dressed," said Helen. Lee asked Mae where Jean was. MaryAnn spoke up and told them that she had business to attend to. Arriving back at the cabin, all the ladies could see that the tables were already set up and the arch was in place. The musicians and caterers were already setting up their equipment. Everyone could feel the excitement in the air. Secret smiled as Royce's car was parked beside some other vehicles.

"Looks like the groom made it," said Helen, rushing her daughter into the house. "You go on and rest. We'll check on your grandmother." Shelia met Secret at the door and helped her get her things to her room.

Jackie escorted Helen, MaryAnn, Mae, and Lee into Hattie's room. "You ladies look so beautiful, and I can't wait to see you in your bridesmaid dresses."

Hattie asked Jackie to raise her bed up. Taking shallow breaths, Hattie said, "I love you all so much because we have been through so much together. I raised each and every one of you, and I am so proud of who you have become. I have left each of you something, and you will forever be in my heart."

Jackie handed each one of Hattie's sisters an envelope but asked them to open it after the wedding. Mae, Lee, and MaryAnn all gathered around Hattie and sang "Amazing Grace." Each gave their big sister a kiss on the cheek and then left the room crying. It was truly an emotional day for them all. Helen just sat in the corner scrolling through her cell phone. She wasn't texting anyone; she was just trying not to fall apart.

"Helen, I consider you my daughter. I want you to know that I never blamed you for killing Lamont." Helen began to weep because she always felt guilty for taking the life of Hattie's only child. "If it wasn't for you, I wouldn't have had the chance to raise Secret. I gave her all the love and strength that I had." Helen couldn't find any words to fit this occasion. She choked on her tears and left the room with a tissue over her mouth.

After a quick power nap, Secret was all smiles as her bridal team unzipped her dream dress. She had no idea what was going on with her grandmother. Everyone else knew that Hattie was within hours of leaving. They had promised Hattie in some way that they would not spoil Secret's big day. The bridal team carefully placed the dress over the excited bride's head.

"You can't look until we say so, okay?" said Thomasia. She placed a large high diamond-encrusted tiara with a beautiful long veil attached upon her head.

"Okay, open your eyes," another attendant said. Secret couldn't believe how stunning she looked. Her first wedding was beautiful, but it couldn't compare to this one. An attendant was right there to dab her face because she already knew that tears were next. "Oh no, Miss Thing, I already said that you cannot cry off all my hard work."

The guests were beginning to arrive from all over town.

Peeping out the back door, Mae asked, "Who are all these people, Lee?"

"Girl, I don't know. I think I recognize a few of them, but they look really old."

"You are old too," said Mae.

"Uh, y'all are old. I'm still young compared to y'all," said MaryAnn. Looking around the room, she asked, "Has anyone seen Jean?" None of the sisters had seen Jean nor had Jackie or Shelia.

Thomasia and her team excused themselves to go check out the fabulous kitchen area. Gina had prepared a table of delicious sandwiches, cheese, fruits, and vegetables for everyone helping with the wedding. Secret sat alone in her cabin room feeling nervous and yet excited. She closed her eyes and thought of her beautiful daughter Destiny. The bride thought of her first husband, Joel Bell, and the love that they shared. He wanted her to be happy even if it wasn't with him. She looked on her beautiful cherrywood antique dresser and found a pen and paper. Looking toward heaven, she felt as if rays of sunshine were beaming on her head. The bride, the mother, the nurse, and the caretaker looked toward heaven. Her words and tears seemed to flow at the same time.

> Dear Destiny, I already know you're doing so good. I can't imagine how much you have grown in heaven. I know that we haven't spoken in a while and I am sorry for that. Mommy has been so busy with a lot of things. Your little brother is here and he looks so cute in his tuxedo. Please tell your daddy that I love him because he gave me you and your brother. Love, Mommy.

Secret smiled as she imagined her daughter running around heaven and her father holding her close in his arms. Instead of feeling sad at what she had lost, she felt comfort in what she had gained. Truly the last chapter of her life had closed, and the next chapter was about to begin.

It was very quiet in the cabin, so Secret decided to check on her grandmother. She creaked open Hattie's door, expecting her to be sitting up smiling. Jackie and Shelia jumped up as soon as Secret walked in.

"Oh my lord, you are the most beautiful bride I've ever seen," said Jackie, elbowing Shelia. "How did you get in here?"

"It was so quiet in the cabin that I just decided to come and check on Granny." Holding up her dress, she tiptoed over to Hattie. Secret's silky lace train was so long until all of it couldn't fit in the door. "Granny, Granny!" Secret bent down and put two fingers on Hattie's wrist. Her heart rate was awfully slow. "Jackie, where is the stethoscope?" Jackie didn't even argue since Secret was actually a nurse practitioner. Listening to Hattie's heartbeat, Secret looked back at Jackie and whispered, "Why didn't y'all tell me?"

Shelia whispered, "Because your grandmother wanted to make sure that your day went smoothly. She made us promise that we wouldn't give you any news that might upset you."

Hattie struggled to open her eyes but did get them open. She struggled to speak, but slowly took shallow painful breaths. "Baby, you look so beautiful. I hope this gift will repay you for all you've done for me." Hattie's clammy shaking hand struggled to touch her granddaughter's tearstained cheeks. "You, my darling, have made all my dreams come true." Thomasia was not there this time to blot the tears in Secret's eyes. Like a waterfall, her tears ran down her grandmother's hands. "I feel so cold," said Hattie, seeming to gasp for her next breath.

"Granny, you've got to hold on just a little while longer. Please, Granny."

"I promise you that I will hold on until after the wedding, "whispered Hattie.

Jackie and Shelia turned around due to a soft knock on the door. "I know this is really bad timing, but the police are here, and they've got Ms. Jean in handcuffs," said Picket.

"What!" asked Secret, trying to run out of the door. For just a minute, she forgot that she had a massive wedding dress on with an extended long train. One of her red stilettos got hung up inside the dress, and she nearly tripped.

"Take it easy, Secret. Let me get your train," said Picket, lifting it up behind her. Walking outside to the front yard, Secret saw three law enforcement officers and her great-aunt Jean standing there crying.

"What in the world is going on here?"

"Ma'am, I am so sorry to disturb your wedding." Holding out his hand, he said, "My name is Detective Allen. This is Sergeant Tilley and Lieutenant King." A loud airplane came flying by, so the detective began talking very loudly. Secret raised her eyebrows but did not shake his hand, so he put it down and kept talking.

"Aunt Jean, what in the world is going on, and why are you in handcuffs? What did you do?" Secret was talking so loud until Mae, Lee, MaryAnn, and Davis all quickly walked outside to see what was going on. Everyone began talking at once. Secret grabbed Davis out of the crowd and took him by the hand. He didn't have a chance to say anything.

Grabbing Davis's hand, Secret whispered, "You're not even dressed, and where is your cane?" She gave him a quick kiss on the lips and squeezed his hand with affection. Davis stood beside Secret but looked back hoping that Royce would come out of the cabin soon. As the detective continued to talk to Secret, Royce came up between them and said, "Sorry, I was in the restroom." Royce leaned in for a kiss from his fiancée, but her mouth was wide open.

"What in the world is going on here, Royce?"

For a brief second, Secret lost focus on the officer and took a double take at Royce and Davis. She wanted to ask him a question but did not have time to even go into it. Picket came outside with Justice and Mercy.

Detective Allen asked, "Whose property is this? We need immediate permission to dig for something."

"Why are you asking about this property? What in the world do you want to dig for way out here?" asked Secret with both hands on her hips. Detective Allen told Secret that there was likely a dead body on the property, and he needed permission to have it dug up. Everyone heard what he said but couldn't believe it. Who was killed and when?

"This is my grandmother's property."

Lee, MaryAnn, and Mae were all shocked to hear that a dead body may be on the property. "Jean, what is going on?" they all asked her at the same time. Jean just held her head down but didn't say a word. She couldn't even look at any of the wedding party.

Detective Allen again focused his attention on the bride. "I need to speak to your grandmother, right now."

"Sir, my grandmother is very ill, and she is not able to speak with you." Just then, Shelia stepped forward and whispered something into Secret's ear. Secret held up one finger and asked the officers to wait for just a minute. Shelia went inside the cabin and searched Hattie's purse. She found a rose-colored envelope and handed it to Secret. Turning around to read the letter, her eyes again filled with tears as she read the letter that Hattie had written her.

> My dearest granddaughter, I love you so much, and I want you to know that the land that you're standing on is all deeded to you. This is your cabin. These are your lakes, your swans, your rose gardens, and all the oil beneath this land. I have already put everything in your name. Please take good care of it and I know you and my grandson will be happy here.

Secret could not believe what she had just read. Enclosed in the letter was the deed to the entire property and a land, gas, and oil deed transferring all mineral and oil rights to Secret.

"Lord Jesus, I can't believe it. This is my property," she said in disbelief. Royce heard what she said, and then he grabbed the letter and read it for himself.

"Excuse me, young lady, what did you say?" She turned back around with a tearful grin on her face. "Ma'am, did you say this is your land now?"

"Yes, this letter and deed says that my grandmother signed it over to me without my knowledge."

The detective asked to look at the letter and deed. "Yes, ma'am, this is all legal, and you are definitely the owner. Well, since you are the owner, do we have permission to dig? I also noticed your name on the big sign driving up here."

"What sign?" The sign had finally been put up right before the wedding, and the new owner had not even seen it.

"There is a huge sign that reads, 'The Secret Hideaway Ranch.'"

"That's another surprise from my grandmother. Royce, what do you think?" asked Secret to her future husband.

He grabbed her hand and whispered, "Babe, whatever it is, we can deal with it. Let him see what they can find. It's obviously very important. We've got to help Aunt Jean." Secret told them to go dig wherever they needed to. All three officers asked everyone out front to please wait patiently inside the home. They didn't want them telling anyone else what was going on with the investigation.

Helen and Shelia went to check on the guests and put on some old-school dancing music. They announced the wedding was running just a little late, but everyone seemed okay to wait. Jean's sisters shook their heads as the officers put her in the back of the police car. With sad eyes, Jean looked back and gave a faint grin.

Thomasia and her team came outside. "Ladies, we've got to go back in the house." Everyone needed a makeup touch-up due to mascara streaks on all their faces. As they walked inside the cabin, Secret grabbed Royce's hand; and through her teeth, she asked, "Royce, did you forget to tell me something?" She raised her shoulders and used her head as a pointer toward Davis. "Which is the better twin? I should have married that one," she said with a smirk.

Before she could answer, Picket walked beside her and said, "I think you got the right twin. I need to investigate the other one." She walked over to Davis and introduced herself.

Royce looked at Picket then cut his eyes toward his bride and whispered, "Future Mrs. Storm, it looks like you forgot to tell me something too. Why is my ex-girlfriend here at my wedding?" Picket got behind Secret and held her train.

"We made peace, and we have an understanding. I'll tell you about that later."

Picket rolled her eyes at Royce but smiled at Davis. Royce rolled his eyes as he could see their connection but didn't say a word. He would be glad to get her out of his hair.

"Secret, I know this is a bad time; but while they are digging for the body, can you see if there is an extra fancy dress in there?" Picket asked quietly.

"Miss Thing, you're not even in the wedding, and you've got that other situation going on."

"I know, but I'm going to make these the best six months of my life. I still got it going on."

"Girl, I can't be mad at that. See that's why we fought so many times, because you are just as strong as I am."

"Secret, I'll fit in the wedding somewhere. I need to see if Thomasia has any extra makeup."

"Ms. Jones, why do you always have the worst timing?"

"It's a gift," said Picket sarcastically. "Now about the dress."

Detective Allen made a call to the cold case investigator. "Hey, Mallory, this is Detective Allen. Listen, I know this is highly unusual, but I need a favor. I have a situation here, and I need your expertise."

"Oh, what is it?"

Detective Allen proceeded to tell the cold case investigator everything that Jean told him about the killing fifty years ago. "I asked my brother-in-law to bring his backhoe on the property. I expect this to be a shallow grave. We're right here digging up the body right now."

"What can I do?" asked Investigator Mallory.

"I know this is probably off the record for now, but can you come and interview the other sisters? They are all elderly now, but I am interested to see if all their stories corroborate each other." Investigator Mallory agreed to come to the property to meet privately with Mae, MaryAnn, and Lee. He also said he'd take a few minutes to see if he could find any information about a missing person in Conway around fifty years ago. He would see what he could find out about a James Ruffins.

Chapter 20

The Wedding This Summer

Although it was somewhat out of order, the guests were allowed to dance and socialize before the wedding started. The wedding party all stayed in the cabin while the officers continued to investigate. A few of Hattie's closest friends were made aware that she was slipping into eternity. They quietly took turns visiting her.

"Ms. Secret, my name is Mr. Patel. I have been close friends with your grandmother for over thirty years. I need to see you immediately after the wedding." Secret was somewhat confused as to who Mr. Patel was and why he wanted to speak with her. In fact, each person who came to say goodbye to Hattie then came by to shake hands with Secret. They all seemed to know her much better than she knew them. What was going on?

Secret and Royce held hands as they sat in the living room of the cabin. He held Mercy on his lap and gave her plenty of kisses. They had been reunited hours earlier while Secret was at the bridal shop.

After Investigator Mallory met with each of Hattie's sister separately, he called his friend Detective Allen with some information. "Allen, all the sisters' stories seem to corroborate with Ms. Jean's story. They still don't know what happened after Mr. Ruffins left his wife, but looks like he was as mean and brutal as she claimed. I couldn't find many records on this guy, but that's not unusual for those times. You've got to remember that around that time, a lot of black people went unnoticed in records. James Ruffins may not have even been his name. He is only mentioned on a courthouse wedding certificate and a birth certificate of a Lamont Ruffins."

"Thanks, Mallory, we found the bones just where Ms. Jean said they would be. I suspect they are indeed the bones of James Ruffins. The poor woman nearly passed out when she saw the bones. Just sit tight until we get back. We are on our way back to the cabin."

There were rumors whispered among the wedding guests due to them noticing a lot of unusual movement going on. Several guests went to see Hattie, several saw the police come out to the yard, and the rest of the guests figured out that the wedding stalled for a while. "What is taking so long?" asked Mae, looking at her watch. Everyone else shrugged their shoulders due to not knowing. Detective Allen and the rest of the law enforcement officers all arrived with Jean out of handcuffs. "Ms. Jean, you can go inside with your family while we discuss the investigation." While inside, everyone hugged Jean as she began to weep.

"Let me get you a seat, Ms. Jean," said Royce.

Jean looked around and said, "Y'all look so beautiful, and look at our baby. Secret, you look amazing. I am so sorry about all of this." She cried. Taking a seat on the couch, everyone in the living room sat down and listened to Jean's entire story of what was happening. Mae, Lee, and MaryAnn felt so sorry for their sister's pain. They had no idea that Jean had killed James Ruffins.

"Jean, does Hattie know?" asked Lee while patting her sister's hand.

"Yes, she knows, and she wants me to let it go. James was a terrible man, wasn't he? Mae, you know better than anyone, don't you?" These two sisters had a secret that the other sisters were not aware of.

Grabbing Mae's hand, Jean cried, "You remember, Mae! He almost . . ."

Mae began to cry. Lee and MaryAnn looked at each other. They both asked, "He almost what? What happened?" Mae told Lee and everyone else in the room that James Ruffins had beaten her until she passed out. He also had other intentions toward Mae, but Jean stopped him right in his tracts. Jean was incredibly quiet, but she was very brave. These sisters had suffered so much and some things they hadn't told each other. Secret, Helen, Picket, and Shelia tried to hold back tears because they could identify with suffering; but the old ladies showed strength and courage.

"Aunt Jean, do you think that you are going to jail?" asked Secret. Jean shrugged her shoulders because she did not know what was going to happen.

The Officers huddled close together as if they were in a football game. "Mallory, let's start with you. What's your take on this?" asked Detective Allen.

"This is a tough one for me, but there is no open or closed cold case on this man. There was never a missing person report. He has no records that he ever existed besides his name on his child's birth certificate. So I don't have anything to work with here. Besides that, the sisters were all eyewitnesses to his abuse of them and his wife."

Detective Allen asked Sergeant Tilley what he thought about everything.

"I know we're not judge and jury here, but I believe Ms. Jean is telling the truth. She did not murder James Ruffins. Looks like it was self-defense to me." Sergeant Tilley said.

"Lieutenant King, what do you say about this?" asked Detective Allen. The men all stood in the front yard of the cabin. They stood in a circle with their backs turned to the peepers out the window.

"What are they saying?" whispered Mae as she struggled to look out the window. Lee couldn't make out what they were talking about.

"Girls, I'm going to jail, and I've messed up Secret's wedding!" cried Jean.

Lieutenant King basically said the same thing as the other officers. "It sounds like the guy had it coming to him."

"That's a good point," said Detective Allen. "Look, I think we should let the old lady go. The funeral director has already been called to remove the remains to another cemetery. His grave will be unmarked. She's been feeling guilty all these years about something that wasn't even her fault." Although none of the officers were the judge or jury, they decided to keep things quiet because they didn't see a case against Jean. There were never any charges filed, neither would there be. Jean wrung her hands as Detective Allen and the rest of the officers told her that she was free to go. She cried and hugged her sisters, then she went and kissed Hattie on the cheek.

Thomasia had been eavesdropping on the entire conversation and rushed in with her team. "Ms. Jean, we've got to get you ready for the wedding." Helen went out and told the guests that the wedding would be starting in ten minutes. All the invited guests had stayed all evening until it was nearly dark outside. Royce, Davis, and Reverend White took their places up front. Gina put on the classic song "My Girl" by the Temptations, in honor of Hattie. Every guest was surprised as Mae, Jean, Lee, and MaryAnn all strode rather slowly down the lighted aisle. These old ladies smiled with their gray hair, wisdom, beauty, and elegance. Each one wore a red and diamond rhinestone crown on top of their heads. They were elderly and beautiful, and the red satin dresses seemed to glisten in the sun. No one had ever seen such elderly bridesmaids, but all the young people witnessed ageless beauty for the first time. The old men were smiling from ear to ear.

"Secret, why are you in here? You should go," whispered Hattie as Secret stood beside her bed. "I know that your future is waiting, and you must walk toward it."

"Granny, you promise me that you will hold on until I get back, okay?"

Hattie moved her feet and began to hum the tune as she could hear all the guests singing "My Girl." Secret gently clutched Hattie's hand and leaned cheek to cheek. They both began to sing "My Girl." Both became teary eyed as Secret said, "Granny, you'll always be my girl."

"And you'll always be mine. I am so proud of the woman that you have become," said Hattie as her lips turned purple. The life was literally draining out of her with every passing second. The wedding march began to play as Secret leaned over and kissed her grandmother. "Granny, I have to go get married, again." They both gave a chuckle.

Thomasia peeked in the room and said, "They're ready for you."

"Okay, I have to go, love, but I will be back," said Secret while releasing Hattie's hands.

"Mother, you look so good. I've missed you so much," said the dying woman.

"Granny, who are you talking to? I don't see anyone."

"Mother is here to take me home. We are going to be with Jesus."

"Don't go, Granny! You promised me that you would hang in there until after the wedding." With all her strength, Hattie reached her shaking bony hand toward a person that no one else could see. Just for a moment, Hattie turned back and whispered, "Baby, I'm so sorry. I made you a promise that I couldn't keep. I love you." Her hand dropped, and her lifeline had been permanently severed.

Secret let out a scream that even the guests could hear. Gina turned off the wedding march, and the entire wedding party ran toward Hattie's room. Everyone held their heads down due to respect. It was painfully obvious that everyone's favorite old lady had finally departed. As the main light in her life went out, Secret locked herself in the room with her grandmother's body. This is not the first time she had felt her mind go dark after she lost someone special. Helen knocked on the door, but there was no answer from inside. "Secret, please open the door. The funeral home is on their way to get the body."

"Granny is gone!"

Helen could feel her daughter's anguish in the tone of her voice. "I know she's gone, but she wanted you to be happy. You have to let her go. Please open the door." The entire wedding party was camped in front of the door. All of Hattie's sisters were crying not only for Hattie, but for the trauma that Secret was going through.

"I hope she is not having a breakdown," cried Jean.

"It seems like all of this is just too much for her," whispered Thomasia to Picket.

"Secret, you've got to come out. The guests are waiting for you. Please come out, sweetie," said Mae.

Secret held her head down and shouted, "I can't go out there! I can't!"

Picket, Secret's aunts, and even her mother tried to talk her out of her hiding place; but she wouldn't budge. Royce was being comforted by Davis in the living room. He was trying to be strong, but he couldn't help but to weep for her pain. Helen grabbed her soon-to-be son-in-law by the hand and pushed him in front of the door. "All right, son, this is your duty. You've got to talk her out of there. The funeral home director just drove up." Royce took a deep breath and knocked on the door.

"Babe, the guests are waiting. You've got to come out. The funeral home just drove up, and they have to take the body."

"I don't care. I can't get married without my granny," cried Secret.

"Honey, do you remember the story that you told me about your grandmother? Your grandmother was the only person who could comfort you after your husband, and later your baby died. She was always there

215

and came with coffee and Kleenex." Royce tapped his finger lightly on the door. Secret gave a slight chuckle and looked at her grandmother's cold dead body. "Didn't you say that she had to dress you like a baby? Then what did you say happened?"

From inside the bedroom, he heard a voice say, "She put my dark shades on and marched me outside the door."

"Oh yeah, that's right." He tried to think of another story that he heard.

"Gina, go make her vanilla coffee and grab a box of Kleenex," whispered Helen. All the aunts followed Gina to the kitchen.

"Remember when you were in college and that guy hit you? Your granny and her sisters tripped him with their canes and beat him up."

Secret chuckled and shouted, "They beat his natural behind!" while wiping her runny nose.

"Babe, I have coffee, Kleenex, and myself. Your grandmother is not here to comfort you, but I'm here, and your family's here. The guests are here, and so is the funeral home director. Every ounce of love, trust, and strength that she put into you is still there. I promise you that I will stand by you through anything. I will be here to wipe your tears." Royce stood there for five minutes not knowing if Secret would respond. The door slowly creaked open.

With a tearful grin, she said, "Royce Storm, do you promise?" There were no dry eyes around the door. The entire wedding party would need a touch-up after this. Royce held out his hand and gave Secret a cup of coffee and a handful of Kleenex. The bride couldn't help but grin.

"Let's go get married," he said.

"Somebody hold my cane." With that said, he gently grabbed her wet face in his hands and kissed her soft lips.

"That's what I'm talking about, brother!" shouted Davis. Royce continued kissing Secret on the lips passionately.

"All right now, save it for the vows," said Reverend White. Everyone laughed, including Secret. "Is everyone ready for this wedding?"

Secret wiped her face and said, "Yes, sir, I'm ready."

Thomasia stepped in between the couple and said, "Excuse me please, I need to fix this beautiful face right quick." Reverend White and the entire wedding party went back and stood in their places. Secret looked back one more time as the funeral home workers removed the dead body out of the cabin. She felt pain, joy, and freedom as she took a deep breath and exhaled. She had to look forward and truly reach for what was now in front of her.

There was no need to start the wedding all over again; too much had happened. However, Helen quickly walked down the aisle throwing out pink, gold, and red rose petals. The grieving bride held her head up even though she wanted to hold it down. She strolled down the beautiful passageway although she wanted to curl up in a ball and disappear. She could hear Hattie say, "Keep going, baby girl, even when everything says run! Stand up to trouble. Face it like the woman that I raised you to be."

Gina started the wedding march again, as everyone stood and looked toward the flower-covered gates. Each lake on the property had been surrounded by red lights. Gina flipped a small switch, and every sparkling light came on. The beauty of the red lights reflected off the water. Picket handed Secret a red rose, white gardenia, and pearl wedding bouquet as she walked out of the cabin. Two ushers opened the gates, and the guests stood up and began clapping their hands. Although clapping was unusual at the start of a wedding, this was no ordinary wedding. Secret had suffered so much over the last few years, and she deserved an applause for her tenacity.

Smiling through her agony, she strode down the aisle that was covered in rose petals. On the side of the aisle were tall crystal vases holding soft white burning candles. A beautiful large gold chain connected each crystal vase to the other. Picket had built a large man-made waterfall full of pink, red, and yellow rose petals at the bottom. The bright white lights could be seen shining through the water. Each tall oak tree had been wrapped in red and white brilliant lights. Truly, Hattie wanted Secret to feel as if she had walked into a dream garden.

The bride focused on her groom as she looked right into his large hazel eyes. She couldn't help but chuckle as she saw an identical pair of hazel eyes standing behind Royce. She couldn't wait to hear the entire story later that evening. The groom had already said his vows behind a closed door, but he repeated them in front of everyone.

Secret wanted to say so many things to the love of her life, but only four words would come out. She placed both of his hands up to her lips and whispered, "Thank you, and I do." The tears in her eyes said it all. That was good enough for Reverend White and for Royce.

This woman was brave, beautiful, and strong. She was all those things because the woman who raised her was all those things. It was truly a beautiful ceremony filled with beautiful scenery, sweet smells, and swimming swans. Although the wedding was supposed to take place earlier in the day, it was dust when it actually happened. Unknowingly, all the lights and candles made everyone feel as if they were in a beautiful fantasy rose garden.

After a long, exhausting, yet beautiful evening, the new couple was anxious to get some rest. The guests would have plenty to talk about once they left the elegant reception. There was a death at the wedding. The police dug up a dead body before the wedding. The bride had a near mental breakdown during the wedding. Everyone talked about the groom doing a romantic rescue on his bride. This wedding and all the events would be the talk of the town for many years.

They hadn't even had a chance to plan a honeymoon due to all the chaos over the last few months.

"Babe, this place is so beautiful. We don't need to go anywhere else," said Royce, kissing his new bride.

"That's true, but everyone is literally here with us on our wedding night," said Secret. They tiredly waved goodbye to the last guest.

"Excuse me, Ms. Bell, I mean Mrs. Storm," said Mr. Patel, looking at the couple. "This was the most intense wedding I have ever been to. I also said goodbye to my longtime friend, Ms. Hattie." Secret gave a faint grin and squeezed Royce's hand. "Hattie instructed me to give you this on your wedding day." Mr. Patel handed Secret a large manila envelope. "I know you don't know me, but I was your grandmother's attorney and estate planner."

"I didn't even know she had money until this weekend," said Secret, pulling out a piece of paper. Without warning, her mouth dropped open, her eyes rolled back in her head, her right arm went up into the air, and she fainted. Her head hit the floor so fast that Royce didn't have time to catch her.

"Babe, babe!" Royce grabbed the paper out of her hand and laid it to the side. Mr. Patel bent down and picked it up while Royce was trying to revive his new bride.

"Here you go. I figured this would be useful," said Mr. Patel, handing Royce a small bottle of smelling sauce.

"What? Granny? What?" Royce helped his new wife back to her feet. She was still wobbly and rubbed her head. "Are you okay, babe? You fell hard."

Mr. Patel just stood there smiling and chuckling. "Mrs. Storm, are you all right?" he asked, handing her the piece of paper.

"Did I see right?" she said, wobbling.

"Babe, please don't faint again." Mr. Patel handed Royce the letter to read. He didn't faint, but he hollered out, "Aww, man!" Not only had Hattie signed over her oil rights to Secret, but she was to receive a check for fifteen million dollars on her wedding day. The money had already been transferred into Secret's bank account. Hattie had left her new grandson a beautiful restaurant close to their new property. Neither could hold back their tears of thanks to a wonderful, thoughtful woman.

"Hattie had a good eye, and as soon as she met you, she had already determined to leave you her restaurant," said Mr. Patel to Royce. "It's called Hattie's Place, and it has some of the best chefs in the state."

The bride and groom embraced each other for what seemed like an eternity. Of course, the entire wedding party had been eavesdropping. Everyone walked out of the cabin smiling and congratulating them.

Mr. Patel looked at each of Hattie's sisters and called each of them by name. "Ladies, oil was discovered on your parents' land many years ago. Although your father was very cruel, he left all the property to Hattie. However, she left each of you a considerable sum of money in the event of her death. You will all be taken care of well beyond your years."

"Somebody turn on some music! We need to celebrate this long, terrible, yet beautiful day!" yelled Jean. Gina put on some old-school dancing music, and everyone formed a line and took turns dancing. Hattie Bell Ruffins was gone, but not forgotten. She had left her name, her fortune, and her courage to the people that she loved most, her family.

"Well, Mr. Storm, I guess we can afford to take that honeymoon after all, can't we?"

"We better take it now because we've got a lot of work to do when we get back," he said. Royce asked Secret where she wanted to go. "I've always wanted to go to Hawaii!"

Helen interrupted, "I know all this is a surprise, so we will take care of the kids. Y'all just go already." There were so many issues to get settled once they returned to Arkansas, but for now they were simply going on vacation. Royce burst out in a loud laugh although no one said anything funny.

"Babe, what are you laughing about?" asked Secret, looking puzzled at her new husband.

"I'm just thinking of a dream that I had months ago. It had fire trucks, oil, mountains, and green grass in it. It was crazy, but I just figured out that all those things came true." Secret asked what made him laugh out loud. "Well, if that dream came true, then maybe my next one will too." Looking at Secret, he said, "I dreamed last night that we were stranded on a desert island living on coconuts."

"Shut up, Royce."

"The funny part was that you were breastfeeding two newborns that had hazel eyes," he said, chuckling. Secret reminded Royce that she had just had a baby last year.

"I know, but they were so adorable," said Royce, sticking his chest out.

"Picket, could you come here for a minute?" Picket walked over and stood beside Secret. "I just need to lean on your shoulder." Secret used Picket as a prop as she took off her red stilettos one by one.

Looking over at Royce, Picket said, "Royce, I think you'd better start running." The bride lifted up her huge ball gown dress, grabbed her red stilettos, and started chasing her new husband around the rose garden.

"Wait, baby, you know I'm on a cane!" Royce was limping as fast as he could.

"I gave you a head start, Mr. Storm!" Secret shouted.

"Look at those two. I've never seen anyone more in love," said Davis while trying not to laugh. Although Royce was trying to run, he wasn't doing too well. "Just let her catch you, brother! It will be easier that way! She's gaining on you!" Davis shouted while shaking his head.

Picket sat down in a chair and said, "Well, there goes those supershoes again. He may not be here long enough for that baby dream to come true."

All the wedding party laughed at the sight of Secret chasing her husband around the rose garden with that huge dress on. She would eventually catch him, and although they didn't know it yet, all their dreams really would come true.

Printed in the USA
CPSIA information can be obtained
at www.ICGtesting.com
LVHW050714100823
754633LV00003B/179